THE ICY WATER SPLASHED IN HER FACE

The shock almost made her cry out, and at that moment the door opened. Instinct took over. Guinevere went as still as a newborn fawn hiding from a predator.

A dim unshielded bulb blinked into life overhead. The man came into the boathouse. Guinevere closed her eyes and told herself she could never get out now. *Damn it, Zac. This is your line of work. You're the one who's supposed to be here in this mess. Not me.*

Another shudder went through her, this time such a mixture of anxiety and cold that she couldn't sort out one sensation from the other. She waited in an agony of suspense, pressing herself flat against the damp planks. If he spotted her, nothing she could say would make her look innocent. It was too late now.

Be sure to read the first Guinevere Jones Novels by Jayne Castle,
THE DESPERATE GAME

Don't miss the next Guinevere Jones Novel.
THE SINISTER TOUCH

THE CHILLING DECEPTION

Jayne Castle

A DELL BOOK

Published by
Dell Publishing Co., Inc.
1 Dag Hammarskjold Plaza
New York, New York 10017

Chapter one first appeared in *The Desperate Game*.

One chapter from a forthcoming book *The Sinister Touch* is
included at the end of this work.

Copyright © 1986 by Jayne Krentz, Inc.

Dell ® TM 681510, Dell Publishing Co., Inc.

ISBN: 0-440-11349-0

Printed in the United States of America

August 1986

10 9 8 7 6 5 4 3 2 1

DD.

THE CHILLING
DECEPTION

Chapter One

Guinevere Jones discovered the gold-plated pistol in the men's executive washroom on the third day of her employment at Vandyke Development Company.

She went back to her desk in Edward Vandyke's outer office and sat brooding about her find for several minutes before she picked up the high-tech stainless steel phone and dialed the number of Free Enterprise Security, Inc. Zachariah Justis's response to the information about the gold pistol was predictable—Guinevere told herself she ought to have anticipated it.

"What the hell were you doing in the men's executive washroom?" he exploded.

"I'll tell you at lunch."

Offended by Zac's failure to perceive the significance of the gun in the bathroom, Guinevere replaced the receiver hard enough to make the listener wince on the other end of the line. The trouble with Justis was that he could be awfully one track; a slow-moving freight train that once started was generally unstoppable.

Guinevere smiled fleetingly to herself as she fed paper into the electronic typewriter. She was looking forward to lunch, even if she would have to spend fifteen minutes of the precious hour trying to explain what she had been doing in the executive washroom.

Half an hour later she arranged for calls to be transferred to another secretary's office, pulled the paper bag containing her new Nike running shoes out of the bottom drawer of the desk, and picked up her purse. Vandyke had still not returned from his strategy session with his managers, but it was twelve thirty, and he had told her to be sure to take her lunch hour on time. A very thoughtful employer.

Darting into the ladies' room halfway down the hall, Guinevere slipped out of her elegant high-heeled gray pumps and quickly stepped into the Nikes. Instantly she felt capable of jogging from the Kingdome to the Space Needle. She breathed a pleased sigh of relief and satisfaction. True, the shoes didn't particularly match the trim gray wool suit she was wearing, but that was of course the whole point.

Guinevere serenely joined several other women wearing suits and expensive running shoes in the elevator and jauntily made her way to the Fifth Avenue entrance of the high-rise building. She spotted Zac's solid compact form before he noticed her approaching. The tiny secret smile she often felt these days when she thought of Zac Justis curved the corners of her mouth. She was growing familiar with the irrepressible flare of pleasure and anticipation that came to life within her whenever she saw him, even though she couldn't fully explain the sensation.

The first time she had seen him she had thought him ugly. A frog, she had called him, and although she had kissed him more than once since that first eventful meeting, Zac Justis hadn't yet turned into a prince.

He wasn't really ugly, but there was something fundamentally different about Zac, Guinevere reflected as she approached him. Standing in the lobby of the office building he seemed separate, removed from the polished males in suits and ties around him. He was wearing the uniform —a dark well-tailored jacket and trousers, crisp white shirt, and subdued striped tie—but he didn't blend into the herd. Perhaps, given the rough unforgiving contours of his face and the remotely watchful quality of his ghost-gray eyes, he would never truly fit in anywhere. Even his dark hair was different. It was cut short, not styled and blown dry. He was a man apart.

In that instant he saw Guinevere, and the remoteness in his eyes disappeared. It was replaced by a disconcertingly direct possessive expression that Guinevere found unsettling. She had been telling herself lately that she ought to discourage that look but she wasn't at all sure how to go about doing it. Deep down she wasn't certain she really wanted to destroy it, anyway. It did something to her when Zac regarded her in that way.

He stood waiting for her, his eyes assessing her neatly coiled coffee-brown hair, wide hazel eyes, and slender figure. She watched his gaze take in the chicly padded shoulders of her jacket, the nipped-in waist that didn't succeed in making her appear bustier than she actually was, and the gray skirt. She knew the very second he saw the new Nikes. Long dark lashes, the only softness in his hard face, lowered deliberately. Then he raised his eyes to meet her faintly smiling gaze.

"Something morbid happen to your shoes?"

"Wearing running shoes outside the office is very fashionable, Zac. It shows a concern for fitness, it's practical for running up and down Seattle's hills during one's lunch hour, and it's subtly, chicly amusing. Besides, they've been doing it in New York for a couple of years."

"That's no excuse. Everybody knows New Yorkers are weird." He shoved the revolving door and guided Guinevere through and out onto the sidewalk.

"You can be very useful to have around," she told him blithely as she buttoned her red coat against the perpetual Seattle mist. The mid-December chill was unrelieved by any sunlight.

"You're so good for my ego." He took her arm as they started across the plaza toward the sidewalk. "Hungry?"

"Always."

"I thought we could flip a coin to see who buys lunch."

"The last two times we did that you won. If we do it again, we use my coin."

"You've got a suspicious nature," he complained.

"Probably comes from hanging around people who conduct investigations for a living," Guinevere agreed cheerfully. "My mother warned me about bad company. How's business? Get that contract to do the security consulting work for that computer firm?"

They had reached the restaurant and Zac held the door open for Guinevere. "I think it's in the bag. Talked to one of the vice presidents this morning, and he wants me to start the project in January. Says his budget can accommodate my consulting fees after the first of the year."

Guinevere shot him a sidelong glance. "Can your budget accommodate the delay in income?"

Zac shrugged one shoulder fatalistically. "It'll have to."

"This isn't a ploy to make me feel anxious about the state of your finances and thus induce me to pay for lunch, is it?"

"Honey, you really have grown more suspicious lately. I'm worried about you."

Before Guinevere could respond the hostess came forward and showed them to a table for two. "We'll go dutch today," Guinevere announced as she picked up her menu.

"You're a hard-hearted woman." Zac bent his dark head to study his menu. "Okay, tell me what in hell you were doing in the executive john."

10

Guinevere chuckled in spite of herself. "I've never seen one before."

"A john?"

"An executive john. Big league, Zac. This is the first time my company has gotten a contract for a short-term secretary to fill in at such a high level. Usually temps are used at lower levels, to fill in for absent clerks. Executive secretaries generally have other executive secretaries in the same firm lined up to sub for them."

"Why did you take the job? Didn't you have anyone you could send out on the assignment?"

"This was the first time Vandyke Development has called Camelot Services for a temp, and I wanted to make a terrific impression. I didn't have anyone I could send who had ever worked as an executive secretary, except my sister Carla. I decided to take the job myself and have Carla baby-sit Camelot Services. She seems to be enjoying running my office lately anyway."

Zac's heavy brows were drawn together in a severe line. "So you raced out to take the job to see what life was like at the top?"

"Zac, we may both be at the top ourselves someday. I for one am going to know what to expect."

"Which was why you checked out the executive head." Zac nodded, satisfied with the interrogation. He put down his menu. "You're lucky you weren't caught."

Guinevere set down her own menu offhandedly. "Mr. Vandyke was tied up in a meeting with his managers. He's been pushing to get a proposal ready and I knew he wouldn't be back in the office until after lunch." She halted as the waitress came by to take their orders. "I'll have the black bean soup and the spicy noodle salad."

"Same for me," Zac murmured. "And coffee—plain coffee. None of that fancy espresso stuff." He waited with vast patience until the waitress had disappeared and began grilling Guinevere again. "Go on. Was it locked?"

"The washroom? Yes. A big gold key on a chain. Mr. Vandyke keeps it beside the door. It's more of a conversation piece than a real attempt to keep people out of the bathroom. His visitors find it amusing. The washroom entrance is a private one just down a small corridor from his office. In fact, you have to go through his office to get to it." She leaned forward, aware of the amused enthusiasm in her own voice. "You should see it, Zac. All black and marble with gold running through it, and mauve."

"Mauve what?"

"Mauve everything. Mauve toilet, mauve washbasin, mauve towels. It's unbelievable. Marble everywhere—walls and floors and countertops. Which was why I happened to notice the gun."

"It contrasted with the marble?"

"No, no, it wasn't on anything marble. It was in the drawer by the sink."

Zac closed his eyes, clearly biting back another lecture. "Jesus, Gwen, you went through Vandyke's bathroom drawers? I knew you were a little light-fingered at times, I found that out during the StarrTech affair, but I never thought—"

"I am not light-fingered!" Incensed, Guinevere straightened in her chair, glaring at him. "Zac, this is important. If you can't listen without interrupting, then I'll—" She broke off abruptly.

He appeared interested. "You'll what?"

"Never mind." She decided to rise above his taunting. Mouth firm, she went on severely. "I noticed one of the drawers was partly open. I happened to glance inside and I could see something gold. So I just sort of eased the drawer out a bit more, and there it was."

"The gun?"

"Yes. And I don't mind telling you, Zac, it gave me a start."

"Maybe it will teach you to stay out of other people's private johns."

The black bean soup arrived complete with a dollop of sour cream in the center, and Guinevere discovered she was too hungry to continue the argument. She spooned up the thick soup with gusto. "Can you imagine, Zac? A gold gun?"

"Probably chosen by the same designer who did the head. Undoubtedly couldn't find one in mauve."

"Zac, this is not a joke."

"Honey, my guess is that it wasn't a real pistol. I'll bet it was one of those gadgets that lights a cigarette when you pull the trigger. Typical executive toy. Your imagination was no doubt in high gear."

"It looked awfully real, Zac." Guinevere became very serious. "And it worries me. Vandyke seems to be under a tremendous amount of pressure."

"You've only been working for the guy for three days. How would you know what kind of pressure he's capable of tolerating?"

She lifted her chin with unconscious arrogance. "I know people, Zac. He's worried and he's stressed."

He shook his head. "You feel sorry for people, you empathize with them. People confide in you because you're a good listener, and you can get along with a wide variety of personality types. That does not mean you 'know' people. Take it from me, Vandyke wouldn't be where he is today if he weren't capable of handling a fair amount of pressure."

"You've never even met the man!"

"Anyone who has a private marble and mauve washroom, let alone a private executive secretary, is basically made of sturdy stuff. Wimps don't get far in the business world."

Guinevere sighed. "You don't understand, Zac. I've been working very closely with him for the past three days. I had to take a phone call from his wife the first morning I was on the job. That call alone was enough to tell me he's on the edge. Vandyke was very upset afterward. And he's been upset every time she's called since."

"He's having marital problems?"

Guinevere nodded. "I'm sure of it. I think she's left him. And I'm sure he's still in love with her. I tell you, Zac, he was in bad shape after those calls."

"So you think he might be planning to kill himself in the executive washroom using a gold-plated pistol. His wife must be something else to warrant that kind of reaction."

Grimly Guinevere pursued her line of logic. "It isn't just the trouble with his wife. I happen to know that the proposal he's working on is a crucial one for the company. He's been wearing himself out getting everything in order for the big presentation to the client next weekend. I think he's afraid of someone stealing the documents. He's instituted very strict security in the office. In fact I think it was security reasons that made him hire an outside secretary instead of borrowing one of the vice presidents' secretaries."

Zac cocked an eyebrow, looking slightly interested at last. "He figured he was safer with an outsider who wouldn't know what she was typing?"

"Or who wouldn't have any contacts in the company. The selection of Camelot Services was probably a deliberately random choice. Vandyke doesn't have to worry about me already having established a foothold in the company as an industrial spy. I don't know anyone in the firm, and no one knows me."

"Your mind is a fascinating thing, Gwen," Zac said admiringly.

"You're not going to take this seriously, are you?"

"Not until I find out what all this is leading up to," he admitted.

Guinevere decided to play her ace. "It could be leading up to a job for Free Enterprise Security," she announced sweetly. "A little something perhaps to tide you over until that consulting assignment in January."

That got another raised eyebrow out of Zac. "What kind of job?"

Guinevere took her time answering. "Well, I'm not exactly sure what you would call it. I haven't discussed this with Vandyke yet either. But I've been thinking . . ."

"Lord have mercy."

She ignored him. "Vandyke is supposed to go to a resort in the San Juan Islands this weekend to make the presentation to his client. I'm going to go with him."

Zac suddenly ceased his methodical attack on the soup. There was an unexpected bleakness in his gray gaze when he looked up. "You're what?"

Guinevere decided not to let his too quiet tone faze her, but it was easier said than done. Her throat seemed to need clearing and her appetite threatened to evaporate. This was idiotic, she lectured herself. Damned if she was going to let Zachariah Justis affect her this way. "Good grief," she managed dryly. "You'd think I had just announced I intended to run off for a quickie weekend fling with the boss."

"That's not what you're announcing?"

"Zac," she hissed, leaning forward, "I am discussing business. The trip to the resort in the San Juans is business. My association with Mr. Vandyke is business. Now if you'll climb down off your macho high horse, you and I will continue to discuss business. If you'd rather sit there and ruin a perfectly good lunch by glowering at me, then I'll let you eat alone."

"Where," he asked bluntly, "do I fit into all this *business?*"

"That's what I was just getting around to explaining."

"I can't wait."

Guinevere drew a deep breath, glad that his eyes had cleared a little. He had no right to react so possessively, she reminded herself. After all, it wasn't as if she and Zac had come to some sort of official understanding about their vague relationship. "I think Mr. Vandyke needs you."

"In what capacity? Chaperone for you and him?"

"Hardly. Mr. Vandyke is nearly fifty and very much in love with his wife."

"Who is presently giving him a hard time."

"Forget Vandyke's wife. I think he needs you to provide him with peace of mind, Zac. I'm going to have a talk with him this afternoon and see if I can't get him to understand that."

Zac looked at her blankly. "Peace of mind? What the hell kind of peace of mind am I supposed to provide him? Is he afraid his wife will find out he's run off to some resort with his new temp secretary? Gwen, you're not making a whole lot of sense."

"I am talking about his peace of mind regarding his proposal documents." Infuriated by his deliberate obtuseness, Guinevere set down her spoon with a snap. "Mr. Vandyke has several things preying on his mind at the moment. I am suggesting that he hire you to take at least some of the pressure off."

"You're going to tell him he should hire me to baby-sit his precious documents? Forget it, Gwen. I'm in the security consulting business, remember? I'm not a file clerk."

"For someone who's not going to see another consulting fee until January you're being rather uppity about this, aren't you?"

"I'm not starving to death. If I find myself in danger of it I'll ring your doorbell and beg for a handout."

"You'd rather beg from me than work for a living?"

A rare, wicked grin spread across Zac's face. "A tantalizing thought, isn't it? What would you give me if I came begging, Gwen?"

"A meal ticket down at the mission! Zac, stop making a joke out of this. I am genuinely worried about my client, and I think I've found a way to take some of the pressure off him and at the same time throw a little business your way."

"A perfect Guinevere Jones solution."

She gave him a challenging look. "Well, isn't it?"

"What do you envision me doing, Gwen? Running around for three days with a briefcase chained to my wrist? Who's going to steal the documents from him at the resort anyway? He's going there to meet the potential client, isn't he?"

"Yes, but he's not the only developer who will be presenting his bids to Sheldon Washburn. There will be two other companies represented. Those executives will undoubtedly be bringing along assistants or secretaries too. Any one of which might be a spy."

"The plot thickens."

Guinevere regarded him with lofty disdain. "Are you interested or not?"

"Not."

She was startled more than anything else. It hadn't occurred to her that Zac would refuse the offer of a job. It was Guinevere's turn to blink. "You mean that? You really don't want to pick up a nice check for three days' easy work?"

"I'm not sure it's good for the image," he said consideringly as their soup bowls were removed and replaced with plates of spiced noodles and chicken. "Briefcases chained to the wrist and all that. Kind of tacky. Smacks of courier boy or something. Low-class."

"I never said the briefcase would have to be chained to your wrist," she muttered. "And since when did you become so concerned with status?"

"You've been teaching me how important image is lately. It's all your fault." He spun a fork around in the noodles, expertly winding them neatly onto it.

Guinevere paused, thrown more off balance by his refusal than she wanted to admit. She'd had plans, she realized. The long weekend at the resort would have provided an opportunity to find some peace of mind for herself. "Well, I suppose if you feel that strongly about it I'll just have to think of something else."

"I not only doubt Vandyke needs a document babysitter on this jaunt, I also doubt he needs a private secretary," Zac went on coolly. "I see no reason for him to drag you along. Tell him your agency does not provide twenty-four-hour secretarial service."

Guinevere's eyes narrowed, resentment beginning to simmer in her. "I run Camelot Services, Zac. I'll decide what jobs to accept."

"Hadn't you better be concerned with your own image?" he shot back too smoothly. "If you get a reputation for taking out-of-town trips with businessmen you might find yourself swamped with more work than you can handle."

Resentment turned to fury, effectively killing her appetite. It took a fierce effort of will to control the angry trembling in her fingers as Guinevere carefully folded her napkin and got to her feet.

"Gwen?" Zac frowned up at her.

"Don't worry, Zac. I won't stick you with my share of

the tab." She coolly slid the money out of her gray leather clutch purse. "That'll take care of my bill with enough left over for a tip. I'll have to trust you not to pocket the tip, of course, but I guess I don't have any choice." She reached for her coat.

"Jesus Christ, Gwen, what do you think you're doing?"

"Walking out before you can insult me any further." She smiled very brittlely. "I'm going back to the office— the man I work for happens to be a gentleman. Gentlemen are so rare these days."

"Damn it, Gwen, I wasn't insulting you. I was just trying to make a point. Now sit down and stop acting like a child. This is ridiculous . . ."

But Zac was talking to empty space. Guinevere had her coat on and was on her way out of the restaurant. In stunned amazement, he watched the scarlet coat flash through the door. Out on the street she turned in the direction of Vandyke's office building and vanished into the crowd. The problem with the new style in women's footwear, Zac decided, was that it allowed the wearers to move a great deal faster than they could in high heels.

Slowly Zac pulled his attention back to his half eaten spicy noodles. "Damn temperamental female."

"Excuse me, sir. More coffee?" the waitress asked with a politely inquiring smile.

"No thanks."

"Will the lady be returning?"

"She had to leave," Zac mumbled, searching for a convenient excuse. It was humiliating to have a woman walk out on you in a public restaurant, he discovered, chagrined. "Business appointment."

"Of course. I'll clear her plate."

"Fine." It would be tacky to tell her to leave Gwen's plate of noodles so he could finish them, Zac decided morosely. Just one more irritation to chalk up to Guinevere Jones, he thought as he watched the excellent noodles disappear toward the kitchen. Not only did Jones abandon him in the restaurant, he couldn't even find a polite way to finish off the food she'd left behind. The lady was getting to him. Zac grudgingly acknowledged to himself that he wasn't accustomed to this level of uncertainty around a woman.

It seemed to him that he'd been alternately irritated, possessive, uncertain, and exhilarated since he'd first encountered Guinevere Jones a few weeks ago. The first time he'd gone to bed with her, he'd been aware of a feeling of rightness that he couldn't begin to explain in words. So he hadn't tried. Their relationship was at a very tentative stage. It could not yet be characterized as an affair, although Zac knew he would be irrationally enraged if he found out she was seeing another man. But surely they had more than a casual dating arrangement. At least, it felt like more than that to him. He'd like to get to the point where he could say he was having an affair with Guinevere Jones, Zac thought. The words sounded good to him. They had a nice, settled, *definite* quality. But as yet he hadn't dared say them aloud in Guinevere's presence.

Words in general seemed to be a real problem around Guinevere. Bleakly Zac finished his noodles and sat cradling his coffee cup in his large hands. Had he insulted her? He hadn't meant to. She must know that. He'd only been trying to point out that weekend jaunts with bosses might be frowned on in some circles—severely frowned on by one Zachariah Justis, as a matter of fact. Damn it, he'd only been giving her some good advice. She certainly spent enough energy giving him advice!

Of course, he reminded himself, perhaps she'd only been attempting to do him a favor. She'd tried to throw a little business his way. He'd been too busy jumping on her for scheduling that weekend trip with Vandyke to pay much attention to the baby-sitting job she'd suggested. Zac stared into his coffee cup and thought about her proposal. Normally the project would not have interested him in the slightest. He had no intention of hiring himself out to ride shotgun for executives who saw industrial spies behind every watercooler. He had deliberately structured Free Enterprise Security, Inc. to be a cut above that sort of mundane operation. His firm was a consulting business. He gave expensive advice, conducted highly discreet investigations, and generally aimed for a sophisticated security image. True, he was still Free Enterprise's only employee, but someday things would change. In the meantime he didn't want to jeopardize the image.

Zac was absently swirling the last of the coffee in his cup and wondering how to go about making amends for insulting her when it struck him that there was one irrefutable advantage to accepting Guinevere's job suggestion. It would enable him to spend a three-day weekend with Gwen at a classy resort.

Three days on an island with Gwen.

Stunned by the implications and wondering foolishly why he hadn't spotted them right from the start, Zac hurriedly fished out his worn leather wallet and matched the amount Gwen had left on the table.

Three days at a fancy resort with Guinevere Jones at the client's expense. It boggled the mind. What was the matter with him? He'd been so damn busy warning Guinevere not to go flitting off with another man that he hadn't even realized she was offering him a chance to be the one she spent the weekend with.

There was the unfortunate matter of having to safeguard a development proposal, but in his new excited mood Zac could anticipate no real problem with that element of the situation. The briefcase would be an annoyance, but he could deal with that. He headed back toward his office wondering if Gwen would let him handle the room reservations.

As soon as he reached the tiny cubicle he rented in the downtown high rise Zac threw himself into the new chair he'd bought with the fee from the StarrTech case, reaching for the phone. Guinevere answered on the second ring. Zac half smiled as he heard what he called her office voice—husky, polite, and just distant enough to let the caller know that the lady was professional in every sense of the word.

"Gwen? Zac. Listen, I've been giving your job offer some more thought."

The polite quality left her voice, but nothing could banish the pleasant huskiness. "Don't strain yourself."

"I'm serious. I've decided you're absolutely right. I can hardly afford to turn down the work. Tell Vandyke that I'll be glad to baby-sit his proposal."

"You will?" She sounded startled.

"Sure. On one condition."

"What condition?" she asked, instantly suspicious.

"No gold handcuffs for the briefcase."

"You want silver or stainless steel?" A thread of humor finally melted the ice in her voice.

"I'll just clutch it with my bare hands. Oh, and Gwen?"

"Yes, Zac?"

He coughed a little, clearing his throat. "Have you made the reservations?" Visions of sharing a room for three days with Guinevere sizzled through his head. He felt his body tighten in instinctive response.

"No, not yet."

"I could handle ours," he offered as nonchalantly as possible.

"You don't have to worry about that, Zac," she assured him breezily. "Vandyke's travel department will handle everything."

"Oh."

Zac hung up the phone, determined not to let the small setback bother him. He would see this as an opportunity to be creative in the field.

Sitting in Vandyke's office, Guinevere stifled the unexpected burst of excitement that threatened to bubble up inside her. This would be a working weekend, naturally, but still . . .

She gathered her wayward thoughts and got to work on the problem of how to convince Edward Vandyke that Free Enterprise Security was just what he needed.

Chapter Two

Late Friday afternoon Guinevere stood at the window of the Camelot Services offices and moodily contemplated the rain that had evolved from an earlier mist. Rain had not been expected to continue into the afternoon, according to the news report. The forecast had been for the morning's light showers to give way to partial clearing. But in typical Seattle fashion the weather had made its own decisions without bothering to consult the local meteorologists. The guy on the evening news would have a brilliant explanation of what had actually happened. In the meantime everyone on First Avenue below Guinevere's window was getting wet.

When visitors asked Guinevere how she tolerated the long gray winters and the frequently damp summers of the Northwest, she was always a bit surprised. Sometimes she responded with statistics proving Seattle's legendary rainfall was actually quite moderate, sometimes she made a joke about having grown webbed feet. But the truth was she rather liked the changeable weather. Normally it was invigorating.

Today, however, the rain seemed intent on complementing her strangely ambivalent mood. She watched the people in the government office building across the street and decided they all appeared to know where they were going and what they were doing. They all appeared to be motivated by a purpose, a direction, a reason for existence. Perhaps they had finally found a way to balance the federal budget. Perhaps they were scurrying around in an attempt to keep themselves *in* the budget. Whatever the reason, Guinevere envied them. Most days she was guided by the same sense of sureness, but not today.

The door of her office opened behind her and Guinevere turned to glance at her sister as she entered. Carla was shaking rain off her fashionable pink and gray umbrella. She looked up, eyeing Guinevere critically, her green eyes speculative. Guinevere wasn't certain she liked the sisterly speculation but it was a great deal more pleasant than the tragic quality that had recently haunted Carla's face. She had recovered from the bout of deep depression brought on by a love affair gone wrong. But nothing would ever completely dispel the air of feminine fragility that Carla wore like an aura. Her blond hair, classically delicate features, and gently molded body made that impossible.

Carla wrinkled her nose in an unconsciously cute movement that called attention to a small sprinkling of freckles. Men were often fascinated by those freckles. They served the function of making an otherwise too attractive woman seem warm and approachable. "For someone who's about to leave on a three-day vacation, you're not looking particularly thrilled with life. What's wrong? Worried about Camelot Services?"

Guinevere shook her head. "Hardly. When I saw what you did to my files I realized the firm was in good hands. Besides, what could go wrong during a three-day weekend? You'll be fine."

"Is that what's worrying you? Am I getting a little too good at running your precious business?" Carla asked the question with a teasing smile, but there was an underlying concern. "The things I do for you are the things any

25

first-class secretary would do. You should know that. You've hired enough first-class secretaries and you've been working as one yourself this past week. I certainly don't want the responsibility of actually owning and operating Camelot Services. I'm not cut out to be the entrepreneurial sort—takes a special breed, and I know it. Some kind of weird cross between a chronic optimist and a chronic worrier."

"Oh, Carla, don't be an idiot." Guinevere grimaced wryly. "I've been grateful for the help and you know that too. I'm fine, really. Just trying to see if I've remembered everything I have to take with me. This isn't exactly a vacation. I'm going to be working."

"Uh-huh. Is that why one of the things you're remembering to take with you is the Frog?"

Guinevere felt the flush in her cheeks, and it thoroughly annoyed her. "Zac is also going to be working on this trip."

Carla grinned cheerfully as she hung up her raincoat. "Sure. Working on getting you into bed. He's only having sporadic success, isn't he? What's the score add up to, four or five times at the most? You've got to admit, he's tenacious. A lot of other men would have decided the game wasn't worth it by now."

The stain on Guinevere's cheeks darkened. "For someone who was only recently having to see a therapist because of a failed relationship, you certainly sound casual about things now."

Carla's gaze softened. "Only because I know Zac is anything but casual in his feelings about you."

Guinevere turned stiffly back to the window. "You wouldn't be so sure of that if you'd heard the way he refused to come along on this trip to the San Juans."

"Is that what's wrong?" Carla demanded. "He isn't going with you and Vandyke after all?"

Guinevere shook her head. "No, he eventually agreed to take the job. But all I got in the beginning was a long harangue about how Camelot Services was starting to appear suspiciously like a rent-a-bedmate agency."

Carla giggled. "Oh, lord, I can just see it now. My heart goes out to the Frog. He put his foot in his mouth by jumping all over you for agreeing to accompany Vandyke, right?"

"Something like that." Guinevere sighed.

"Then he finally realized you were offering him a vacation fling with you, and had to backtrack like mad. Must have been painful for him."

"It wasn't exactly pleasant for me either. I thought he'd jump at the chance to go with me," Guinevere said wistfully. "Instead all I got was a lecture, until he finally realized he shouldn't turn down the job. Zac doesn't have any major consulting projects scheduled until January. Apparently he decided he could use the work. How do you think I feel, knowing he's only coming along for business reasons?"

"If you think that, you're not bright enough to be running Camelot Services."

Guinevere glanced up, eyes narrowed. "Well, how would you interpret it?"

Carla sat down behind Guinevere's desk. "Simple. His initial reaction was sheer jealousy. It was only after he'd calmed down a bit that he realized you were offering him a weekend fling."

"I am not offering him a weekend fling, Carla!"

"Then you can't blame him for going with you purely for business reasons, can you?"

Guinevere groaned and leaned her forehead against the cold glass. "It must have been a lot easier in the old days. Back when a woman could simply ask a man if his intentions were honorable."

"Men lied in the old days as easily as they lie today." Carla's voice was laced with memories of her own recent experience. "Besides, the definition of 'honorable' has changed. It used to mean marriage. Is that what you want?"

"I've only known him a few weeks!" Guinevere said with barely suppressed desperation. "Of course I don't want to get married. I don't want to marry anyone. You know that. I've got my hands full putting this business on its feet and I've gotten very used to my independence. I like being my own boss, Carla, both in business and in my private life."

"Okay, so you don't want marriage. What do you want?"

"Damn it, *I* don't know. I just know I don't like this foggy, undefined kind of relationship. I'm a businesswoman. I like things clear-cut, rational, comprehensible. He's a businessman. I thought he'd want the same clarity in his personal life."

Carla's mouth curved gently as she studied her sister. "What would make your relationship with Zac clear-cut, defined, and rational?"

"I wish I knew." Guinevere thought about the question. What did she want from Zac? "I just wish I knew." She straightened away from the window, forcing a determined smile. "And on that note, I guess I'd better go home and pack. Vandyke wants to leave first thing in the morning."

"You're really concerned about him, aren't you?" Carla asked shrewdly. "Not good to get emotionally involved with a client, Gwen. No wonder Zac was annoyed when you announced you were running off to the San Juans with Vandyke."

"I'm not emotionally involved," Guinevere said bluntly. "Not in the way Zac first thought. But yes, I am worried. You would be too, if you saw Vandyke. He's tense and nervous, constantly drinking coffee and making little notes to himself. This proposal is a big one for his company. On top of that he's got problems with his wife."

"Have you met her?"

"No. But I've answered the phone every time she's called. And she calls him every day. I can't figure it out. She sounds so lonely, so unhappy. Vandyke sounds the same way when he finishes his conversations with her. But if they're both lonely and depressed being apart, why on earth *are* they apart? Mrs. Vandyke seems pleasant enough, but what can you tell on the phone? At any rate, I figured if Vandyke could at least stop worrying so much about somebody trying to steal his proposal documents, he might be able to relax sufficiently to make a good presentation to Washburn this weekend."

"Zac is supposed to guard the documents?"

"That's what I suggested to Mr. Vandyke." Guinevere went to collect her coat and shoulder bag. "He wasn't too keen on the idea at first, but I gave him a really brilliant presentation of my own."

Carla glanced up warily. "How brilliant?"

"Well, I convinced him that Zac was the best private security to come along since James Bond. I painted quite a glowing picture of the intrepid man of action. Vandyke finally seemed to think it would be a good idea if he hired Zac."

"Does Zac know about your little sales job?"

Guinevere shrugged into her coat. "Naturally, I didn't tell him in detail what I said to convince Vandyke," she said lightly. Discretion was the better part of valor in this instance. Zac would have been furious if he'd found out what a swashbuckling image he now had in Vandyke's eyes. "But Zac seems happy enough with the idea of the job now."

"Have Zac and Vandyke met?"

"Yesterday, in Vandyke's office." Guinevere paused, remembering the meeting. It had gone fairly well. Vandyke had asked Zac several questions about his past work and had seemed satisfied with the answers. Alone with Guinevere Zac had been downright casual about the job, but he'd managed to put on a politely concerned front in Vandyke's presence. He'd agreed to go along in the role of Vandyke's personal assistant.

"Well, sounds as though it should be an interesting weekend," Carla decided. "Have fun. I'll see you Tuesday morning. Maybe by then you'll have achieved clarity, rationality, and a sense of definition in your relationship with the Frog."

"Why is it that sounds like a contradiction in terms?" Guinevere asked as she went out the door.

Saturday afternoon Guinevere again stood at a window watching an endless rain. But, she reflected, this time she at least had the advantage of standing in a luxurious hotel room, and the view was of tiny mist-shrouded islands dotting a stormy sea rather than clock-watching government office workers. The dozens of green islands off the coast of Washington that made up the San Juans comprised an exotic bit of Northwest paradise. The ferry system serviced the larger islands, such as the one on which the resort was located, but most of the smaller islets were accessible only by private boat or seaplane. Many were tiny and uninhabited. It was even possible to own your very own island. Guinevere smiled briefly at the thought. Her very own island. Now that was class. Almost as good as having one's own executive washroom.

The phone beside the bed rang. She gave a small start and went to answer it.

"Are you unpacked?" Zac asked without any preliminaries. His temper had been a bit unpredictable since their arrival that morning, and after he'd discovered he'd been given a room next to Vandyke and that Guinevere's room was several doors down the hall, he'd begun to show signs of grave uncertainty.

"Just finished. Vandyke said he wouldn't need me until after this afternoon's meeting with Washburn. How about you?"

"I finally convinced him that the documents were safe enough with him during the meeting." Zac sounded distinctly irritable. "Hell, I thought he was going to make me accompany him right into the sessions with Washburn. I told him I'd be standing by to collect the documents at four o'clock, when the meeting is scheduled to end. When I pointed out that not much could happen as long as he was closeted in the hotel conference room he reluctantly agreed. The guy really is a nervous wreck, isn't he? I wonder if Vandyke Development is in some sort of financial trouble."

"I wouldn't know. I've only worked for him a week. But I agree the poor man's on the verge of a severe anxiety attack."

"Yeah. Well, that's his problem, I guess. I'm not licensed to prescribe tranquilizers. What do you say you and I get out of here for a couple of hours. We can take a walk."

"In the rain?"

"Unless you can think of another way to take a walk today."

Guinevere held the phone away from her ear for a moment, glaring at the receiver. "I'll take a walk with you if you'll promise to remain civil," she said into it again. "You've been acting like a frustrated buffalo ever since we arrived."

"Frustrated may be the key word. I'll pick you up in five minutes. Somebody must have worked hard to find you a room as far away from mine as possible. It couldn't have happened by sheer luck."

The phone clicked in Guinevere's ear. Slowly she hung up, thinking about Zac's mood. He definitely sounded annoyed because the Vandyke travel department hadn't put her in a room next to his. Well, perhaps it was better this way. She hadn't intended these three days to be a sexy vacation fling. She envisioned instead a series of intense meaningful discussions. After all, she wanted to clarify the relationship.

Zac showed up four and a half minutes later. He had a waterproof windbreaker on over a heather-colored wool sweater and casual slacks. His eyes were the same color as the rain, Guinevere realized in faint surprise as she opened the door.

"Be ready in a second." She reached for her rakish red trench coat, belting it on over her pleated khaki pants and green pullover sweater.

"Trench coats are supposed to be khaki," Zac noted.

"You're such a traditionalist."

"At least you've found something else to wear besides sneakers." Zac eyed her fashionable rain boots.

"So glad you approve," she retorted coolly as she walked out the door with him.

Zac hesitated and then took her arm. "Sorry," he muttered. "I didn't mean to snap at you."

Guinevere heard the sincerity beneath the rough apology. "Perhaps Vandyke's tension is rubbing off on you," she suggested.

"Nope. That's not it at all."

"I see."

"Let's take the car into the village. We can walk around there. Maybe have a cup of coffee and look at the marina."

"Okay." Relieved that he wasn't going to launch an in-depth discussion concerning the reasons for his short temper, Guinevere allowed Zac to guide her out into the parking lot. He and Vandyke had each brought their own cars on the ferry. Vandyke's was a new Mercedes. Guinevere had come with Zac in his three-year-old Buick.

The small village, crammed with tourists during the summer, was quiet on a rainy winter weekend. It was easy to find a parking space near the marina and even easier to get a cup of coffee at a nearby café. Guinevere sensed Zac relaxing a little as the time passed.

"This is more what I had in mind," he announced as they left the café.

"Really?" Guinevere glanced up at him with a tentative smile. "Could have fooled me. I thought you were opposed to this trip."

His arm tightened around her shoulders. "Only until I started thinking of the possibilities." He started to say something else and then halted, glancing at a man who was opening a car door across the street. "Isn't that Springer?"

Guinevere peered through the rain at the young man dressed in slacks and a suede jacket. "I think so. I only met him once this morning after we arrived. He's Washburn's assistant, isn't he?"

"Yeah. Guess they decided they didn't need any extras at the first meeting. Looks like he's headed for the marina. Maybe he's got a boat."

Ambling along in Toby Springer's wake, Guinevere and Zac watched the man make his way past the rows of boats tied up in the marina. He was headed toward an old tin boathouse at the far end of the wharf. A single-engine seaplane bobbed on floats in the water next to the boat-house. Near the plane another man was crouched down over a twist of rope on the dock.

He must have said something to Washburn's assistant, because in the next moment Springer turned and saw Zac and Guinevere. He waved invitingly.

"I'm not interested in a ride in that silly little plane," Guinevere hissed to Zac as he started forward purpose-fully.

"You'll love it."

"Not a chance."

"Come on, Gwen, where's your spirit of adventure?"

"It hasn't recovered from the StarrTech case. It may never recover."

Zac wasn't paying any attention. He was busy greeting Washburn's assistant. "I see you escaped for the after-noon too. I was afraid for a while there that I'd have to sit in on the meeting."

Springer laughed, nodding politely at Guinevere. He was a clean-cut man in his mid thirties with well-styled hair, designer clothes, and a sense of his own future worth. But he was also very charming. "I know what you mean. When Washburn told me we were getting three days in the San Juans I knew there were going to be a few catches. How are you, Miss Smith?"

"Jones," Guinevere corrected automatically. "I'm fine. Zac and I decided to sneak off for a tour of the town. I just love islands in winter."

"Personally," growled a soft masculine voice behind her, "I prefer other islands in winter. Islands with plenty of sun and sandy beaches. This sure as hell isn't my idea of paradise," Laconic, laid back, slightly world-weary and coolly cynical, the voice contained a hint of a South-ern drawl. "A man who got himself stranded on one of

34

these little uninhabited rocks in winter would probably wake up dead."

Guinevere turned. Although Zac was merely glancing back over his shoulder in response to the new voice, his fingers tightened a bit on her upper arm as he eyed the speaker. The man who had been crouched over the coils of rope was getting slowly to his feet. Guinevere watched him rise, admiring the perfection of a legend brought to life. A slow smile lit her eyes. It wasn't every day a woman got to see this sort of thing in the flesh.

The man rose to his full height. He must have been at least six one. Maybe six two, she decided. And he could have stepped out of an adventure film. More particularly, a film featuring a dashing, raffish, danger-loving pilot with plenty of "the right stuff." He was even wearing a genuine beat-up leather flight jacket complete with a scruffy fur-lined collar. His khaki pants were tucked into worn, scuffed boots and there was a wide leather belt around his lean waist. As she watched he very coolly stripped off his leather gloves and extended a hand to her. It was a picturesque gesture.

"The name's Cassidy," he drawled, blue eyes running over her in slow appraisal. He appeared to be in his mid forties, but his dark brown hair was still full and had just the right touch of shagginess. His face was as lean and hard as the rest of him.

Entranced, Guinevere put out her hand and immediately felt the strength of his grip. "Cassidy," she repeated. Even the name sounded perfect. "My name is Guinevere. Guinevere Jones."

"I wish to hell my name was Lancelot." His eyes ceased their perusal and he met her gaze, grinning. "Lancelot was the one who finally got Guinevere, wasn't he? My history's a little rusty."

Zac's fingers were definitely digging into Guinevere's

shoulder now. She moved slightly, trying to encourage him to loosen his grip, but he didn't seem to notice. "It wasn't history. Just a story," he responded to the other man's comment. "Nobody ever gets the facts right in those old stories."

Cassidy switched his gaze to Zac. He shrugged good-naturedly and held out his hand again. "I get the picture. Don't worry, I know private property when it's marked."

"I'm glad. Zachariah Justis." He accepted the other man's hand, ignoring Guinevere's gathering irritation. The handshake was polite but short. Neither man seemed anxious to prolong the civilities. "You fly the San Juans?"

"I do a little charter work."

Zac nodded toward the bobbing plane. "The One Eighty-five is yours?"

"Yup." Cassidy smiled in bland satisfaction. "Me and that Cessna have been through a lot together. But I don't think she's any more used to this cold weather than I am. Guess we haven't gotten acclimated."

"Where were you before you came here?" Guinevere asked interestedly. She would speak to Zac later about his rudeness, she decided.

"Worked the South Pacific," Cassidy said. "Sight-see-ing trips for tourists, a little mail, some cargo. You name it. Thought it was time for a change, so I threw some darts at a map and came up with the San Juans. Soon as I got a taste of that cold dark water I began to have doubts."

"It's cold, all right," Guinevere agreed. "Hypothermia is a real problem around here in boating accidents. During winter a person can't last long in the water."

Cassidy sighed. "Back where I come from a man could swim from one island to another as far as those out there and feel like he was in a bathtub the whole way." He indicated the handful of mist-shrouded islets in the distance. "But around here a pilot's got to carry all kinds of survival gear just in case he does something dumb and winds up in the water."

"Hey, don't go into a long lecture on the perils of flying the San Juans, Cassidy," Toby Springer interrupted with a laugh. "I'm down here to see about arranging some tours for Mr. Washburn's guests. Gwen and Zac here are two of your potential passengers. Be careful, you'll scare them off."

Cassidy grinned engagingly, his eyes dancing over Guinevere. "Well now, I surely wouldn't want to risk that. Don't you worry about a thing, Miss Jones. I'll keep you nice and warm during the whole flight."

"Gwen doesn't like flying in small planes," Zac said smoothly, conveniently forgetting his earlier comments regarding her lacking spirit of adventure.

Cassidy looked crestfallen. "Ah, hell, I didn't mean to scare you off, Gwen. Safe as houses up there. That old Cessna practically knows how to fly herself by now."

"A cheerful thought. Just the same, I think I'll do my touring by boat or on foot. Zac's right. I'm not big on dinky little planes."

"Dinky!" Cassidy was theatrically offended. "That One Eighty-five is a real workhorse. She can carry six passengers, or a whole mess of cargo."

Guinevere laughed. "I didn't mean to insult the plane. Have you been a charter pilot for long?"

"Since I got out of the army. A long time, Miss Jones. More time than I want to add up." He stepped around her to where he'd coiled the rope, and as he moved Guinevere saw he had a distinct limp. She just knew there would be a good story behind that limp. Old war injury? Plane wreck? Enraged husband? "Hope you change your mind about flying with me, Gwen," Cassidy went on easily as he bent down to collect the rope. "I'd sure love to show you the sights."

"I'll bet," Zac muttered. "Come on, Gwen, it's getting late," he added more loudly. "I promised Vandyke I'd be back by four." He nodded crisply at Cassidy and Springer. "We'll see you later."

"Right," Springer agreed. "Probably in the bar. Good-bye, Miss—uh, Jones."

"Good-bye, Mr. Springer." She didn't have a chance to do more than nod briefly at Cassidy. Zac was already hauling her back along the plank dock. "Zac, what's the rush? It's only three thirty."

"Somehow," Zac observed caustically, "I get the feeling the entire world is conspiring against me."

"Sounds like a clear case of paranoia."

"All I know is, this trip isn't turning out to be what I expected."

"You have to be flexible, Zac."

But all Zac seemed intent on flexing at the moment was a little muscle. Guinevere found herself back at the Buick before she had a chance to catch her breath. Turning to glance once more toward the marina she saw Springer in deep conversation with the man called Cassidy.

It was during dinner, which she and Zac shared with Edward Vandyke at his insistence, that Guinevere learned she was not alone in her dislike of small planes. Vandyke fully concurred with her feelings.

In the week she had known him Guinevere had come to like the slightly balding, slightly paunchy, earnest, hardworking Vandyke. She knew there was intelligence and ambition beneath the sincere manner, as well as a willingness to work hard for his objectives, and she admired that. As she sat across from him at the dinner table

38

she wondered what was causing the anxiety she sensed eating him. It seemed out of proportion to the business he was here to negotiate with Sheldon Washburn.

Washburn, a thin well-dressed man in his fifties, and his assistant Toby Springer were seated on the other side of the dining room. The two other businessmen and their assistants who were there to make presentations to Washburn were also eating. Everyone had been quite civilized over cocktails earlier, Guinevere reflected in amusement. You'd never know from looking at them that there was so much money on the line, she thought.

"I know exactly how you feel, Miss Jones," Vandyke said in response to her comment about seeing the small plane in the marina. "I did some charter work myself in my wild and misspent youth. It would suit me perfectly never to get near anything smaller than a Seven Twenty-seven again in my life."

Zac prodded his red snapper. "You did some flying?"

Vandyke nodded. "At the time it seemed very adventurous and it certainly made for some great cocktail stories over the years. But to tell you the truth, most of what I remember is the unpleasant aspects. Running a shoestring charter service is no picnic. Still, I suppose I shouldn't complain. It provided me with the stake I needed to start Vandyke Development."

"Did you operate alone?" Guinevere asked.

Vandyke concentrated on his salad. "No. I had a partner for a while. There was an accident, and he was killed. It was one of the things that made me decide I'd pushed my own luck far enough. I was sick of flying around, under, and through tropical storms; landing on dirt roads, or in places where there weren't any roads at all; trying to collect for deliveries from people who could have cared less about their credit ratings. And then Gan-

39

non got himself killed. . . ." Vandyke paused for a long moment, his dark eyes distant and full of fleeting pain.

Empathic as usual, Guinevere immediately wished she hadn't asked the question. Zac, however, seemed oblivious of Vandyke's unhappiness. Tearing off a chunk of sourdough bread, he asked, "Tropical storms? Where did you do your flying?"

"The Caribbean. What about you, Zac? Has your varied background included a bit of flying?"

Zac shrugged. "Some. Not much. It was a long time ago."

"Ever yearn to go back to it?"

"Nope. I feel the same way you do. For me the old adage applied: hours of boredom broken by moments of stark terror. Basically I'm a quiet businessman at heart. I prefer to—ouch!" He glowered at Guinevere, who had just kicked him under the table.

Guinevere smiled sweetly at Vandyke, who was looking curiously at Zac. "Zac tries to downplay his more adventurous activities. He's always pretending that everything he does professionally is just business as usual. Actually, some of his tales make your blood run cold. But you have to get him fairly drunk before you get the truth."

Vandyke managed a small chuckle. "I see. I'm not surprised. I suppose most men who have lived action-oriented lives like yours, Zac, become very casual about the risks they take."

"Until they get kicked under the table," Zac muttered.

"Well, I for one am very glad I took Miss Jones's advice and hired you to come with us this weekend. I shall sleep a lot better knowing you're nearby in case of need." Vandyke paused. "Do you carry a gun, Zac?" he asked in a low tone.

Guinevere jumped in to answer before Zac ruined the

image she had so carefully created. "Of course he carries a gun, Mr. Vandyke. But he prefers not to mention it at the dinner table."

"I understand."

"I'm glad somebody does," Zac observed.

Later, after joining the others for a nightcap in the lounge, Zac decided he'd done his social duty. The first day of his long weekend with Guinevere was almost over, and thus far it had offered such highlights as an aging macho pilot in a Goodwill flight jacket who had made a pass at Gwen, dinner with a man who had a hard time hiding his personal anxiety beneath a layer of business charm, the discovery that Guinevere's room was quite a ways down the hall from his own, and a bad choice of wine at dinner. The last had been Vandyke's fault, but since the older man was picking up the tab it had seemed crass to complain. Zac had kept his mouth shut and gone back to tequila as soon as dinner was over. You were always safe with tequila.

A roaring fire burned on the huge hearth in the resort lounge. The businessmen who had gathered at the hotel were well into a late-night drinking siege and Guinevere was beginning to look pleasantly sleepy. It was definitely time to go back to the room. Zac reached out to touch her hand.

"Let's go, honey. It's late, and you're half asleep."

"Okay," she agreed easily enough. Smothering a small yawn, she obediently got to her feet and said a polite good night to Vandyke, who glanced up and then rose.

"You two are going to your rooms?" he murmured, looking directly at Zac.

"That was the plan." Zac arched one brow inquiringly. "Any objections?"

"No, no, of course not. I just wondered . . . That is

. . ." Vandyke coughed a little in embarrassment and leaned forward confidentially. "Look here, Zac, I hired you to keep tabs on, uh, things. I hate to sound priggish, but the fact of the matter is I would appreciate it if you stayed in your own room tonight. So I'll know where to find you if I need you."

"I hadn't planned on leaving the hotel." Zac shot a sidelong glance at Guinevere, who was saying good night to Toby Springer. She couldn't hear what Vandyke was saying. "Don't worry, Mr. Vandyke. I'll keep tabs on your briefcase."

"Yes, well, thank you, but I'd like to know where you are at all times. Do I make myself clear?"

Zac thought of the connecting door between his room and Vandyke's. It was locked, naturally, but that didn't mean much. The resort was old, the walls badly insulated. A man on one side of that goddamn connecting door would certainly be able to hear any sounds made by the occupant of the other room. A woman's soft cry of passion would be unmistakable. And Guinevere had her image to maintain. She wasn't likely to make love within earshot of her current client.

Without a word Zac took the precious briefcase from Vandyke, collected Guinevere, and left the lounge.

It occurred to him that maybe it was time to find out what it was about the development proposal being presented to Washburn this weekend that made Vandyke so damn edgy. The man was acting as if he needed a bodyguard, not just a baby-sitter for important papers.

Chapter Three

"What do you mean you're going to have a look in the briefcase? You can't do that, Zac. Those are my client's private business papers. Besides, it's locked." Guinevere shut the door to her room as Zac strode across the carpet and set the briefcase down on the bed.

"He's my client too. Remember? And he's acting weird."

"I told you he was very anxious about a lot of things."

Zac crouched down in front of the briefcase to study the locks at eye level. He fished a paper clip out of his pocket and straightened it. "He was the one who had the hotel give me a room next to his, Gwen. With a connecting door, no less. I asked the desk clerk this afternoon if there was any way of getting a different room, and was told that the present arrangements were per Mr. Vandyke's personal request. And just now Vandyke ordered me to sleep in my own room."

Guinevere flushed. "Yes, well, perhaps he was just trying to look after me. He's very much a gentleman, Zac. He might feel obliged to, er, protect me from unwanted advances. Or something."

"Bullshit. Vandyke is making it clear he wants a bodyguard, not a baby-sitter. But he won't come right out and say it. I'm starting to get curious." Zac fiddled delicately with the locks on the briefcase. "He's not as concerned about where the briefcase is as he is where I am. He was upset this afternoon when he got out of his meeting early and found us gone. I got the feeling he expected to find me standing right outside the front door of the conference room with my trusty machine gun slung over my shoulder."

"Maybe he has a right to be upset." Guinevere went to stand beside Zac, eyeing his efforts curiously. "After all, he is paying us to be on call this weekend. Where did you learn to do that?"

"Correspondence school." There was a tiny ping, and one of the locked clasps sprang open. Zac turned his attention to the other.

"Amazing what you can learn at home these days." Guinevere leaned closer. "Is it hard?"

"Only when someone's breathing over your shoulder."

She leaned closer. "You have to learn to work under pressure, Zac."

"Pressure," he announced as the second clasp popped open, "is something I'm learning a lot about this weekend."

"We've only been here one day."

He opened the briefcase. "Don't remind me." He stood up and examined the contents. Folders, several thick documents with *Vandyke Development Proprietary Information* stamped all over them, and a number of letters were neatly arranged in the case. There was also a small silver flask tucked into one corner. Zac reached for it.

"You didn't tell me the guy was a closet drinker." He unscrewed the top and sniffed. "Cognac."

"He has been under a lot of pressure lately, as I keep reminding you. Maybe he feels the need of a nip now and then, how should I know? He certainly handled his alcohol all right this evening." She broke off consideringly.

44

"Of course, it would have been hard to drink very much of that wine at dinner."

Zac replaced the flask. "You can say that again. Tomorrow evening we'll have to work it so that one of us gets to choose the wine."

"It'll have to be me. Anyone whose regular fare is tequila can't be trusted to pick good wine." Guinevere carefully probed the contents of the briefcase. "I've seen most of these at one time or another during the past week. He had me do some of the final revisions. He didn't even want some of these documents sent out to the word processing pool."

"That's a normal precaution when there's a major deal at stake. Routine company security." Zac lifted out a few of the papers and set them on the bed. "But Vandyke isn't acting routine."

Guinevere examined a cost analysis. "Are you sure you're not overreacting because he as good as ordered you to spend the night next door to him instead of, uh, wandering the halls?"

"Wandering the halls," Zac repeated thoughtfully. "Is that what you call it?" He didn't wait for an answer. "Let me see that envelope."

Obediently Guinevere handed it to him, watching as he opened the manila envelope and drew out a single sheet of paper. It was a badly photocopied document, she saw. Head tipped to one side, she peered at the grungy gray page. "That wasn't done by me. I would never have accepted such a bad print. In fact, I don't think the printing department at Vandyke Development would let any of the machines get that bad. They keep them in excellent condition."

Zac held it up to the light. "It was done on one of those cheap little machines you sometimes see installed in out-of-the-way places. You know, the kind of store that sells gas, cigarettes, condoms, and booze."

"A real service-oriented sort of place." Guinevere tried to get a look at the page. It appeared to be a form that had had various blanks filled in by hand. There was a column of scrawled names with spaces opposite for times and dates. At the bottom there was a signature. "What is it, Zac?"

He studied it thoughtfully for a long moment. "A page out of a pilot's logbook," he told her absently.

"No kidding? Let me see." She reached for the paper and he handed it to her. "These are the destinations? The places he flew? And these are the times and dates?"

"Yeah."

"I don't recognize too many of these towns."

"That's because most of them are names of places in the Caribbean and the West Indies." Zac peered over her shoulder. "The dates are all from nineteen seventy-two. The last one is May ninth. It says the pilot made a round-trip from Saint Thomas to some little island off the coast of South America. The trip back to Saint Thomas apparently took place several weeks after the trip out. Let's see . . . the first hop was in April. The return trip was on May ninth."

"Vandyke said he used to have a charter service down there some years ago. But that's not Vandyke's signature at the bottom of the page." Guinevere was positive of that—she'd seen her client's signature on enough papers during the past week to be certain. "It's hard to read. Shannon? Bannon?"

"Gannon," Zac said suddenly with finality. "L. Gannon." He took the paper back from Guinevere with a snap and replaced it in the envelope. "That was the name of the man Vandyke said was his partner, remember? The guy who got killed in an accident."

Guinevere shuddered. "It seems morbid to carry that kind of keepsake around, doesn't it? After all these years, I wonder why he does?"

"You'll notice he's not carrying around the original." Zac shoved the envelope back into the briefcase and replaced the rest of the documents. He relocked the case.

"So?"

"Don't look at me like that. I don't know the answer. All I know is that I'm being asked to stick very close to a man who's on the verge of having an all-out nervous breakdown."

Guinevere sat down on the edge of the bed, staring out the window. She could hear the rising wind heralding an incoming storm. "I'd hoped having you along would calm him down a bit, but it doesn't seem to be working. He's under so much pressure, Zac. I feel sorry for him."

There was silence behind her and then the lights went out as Zac flipped the switch. Guinevere didn't move, although she felt a sudden surge of tension. With the room lights off the gardens outside the window were faintly revealed by the discreetly placed outdoor lighting.

A moment later the bed gave beneath his weight as Zac sat down beside her. She hadn't heard him cross the room, but that didn't surprise her. When he wanted to, Zac could move very quietly. He reached out to fold her hand into one of his.

"How about feeling a little sorry for me, Gwen."

"Is it sympathy you want from me?"

He exhaled heavily. "No, not really. But I am suffering."

"Are you?"

"This trip isn't going quite the way I had imagined it would. Christ, I feel like Cinderella. I've got to be back in my own room by midnight or Vandyke will be pissed."

Guinevere turned her face against his shoulder. "I'm

sorry, Zac. I sort of hoped it would be different too," she confessed tremulously. His arm tightened around her and she could feel the welcoming strength in him.

"Did you?"

Mutely she nodded, her face still tucked against his shirt. She loved the warm male scent of him, she realized. There was something comforting and deeply intriguing about it. She felt him reach up to loosen his tie, and then he cradled her face in his palm.

"I'm glad, Gwen."

His mouth came down on hers, heavy and warm. Guinevere shivered and let her fingers creep up around his neck. This wasn't quite the way she had planned it, she reminded herself. She had wanted them to talk this weekend to get a few things out in the open. A part of her needed to analyze the relationship that was growing between herself and Zac, and she had hoped that a quiet resort might provide the right atmosphere for that kind of delicate discussion.

The sensual side of their association was already powerful enough. On the few occasions when she had allowed it to take the dominant role Guinevere had had plenty of proof of that. Zac's effect on her senses was almost overwhelmingly intense. The passion sprang up so easily between them. Guinevere was starting to worry that it came too easily. She had been trying to keep it in perspective, not allow it to take over.

"Gwen, honey, I've been aching for you all day. We have a little time. Vandyke's probably still down in the bar. . . ." Zac's soft murmur was charged with sexual tension. The urgency he was feeling was being clearly communicated to her. Guinevere felt his hand against the sensitive nape of her neck. His fingers slid around her throat to the buttons of her yellow silk blouse.

"Zac," she whispered huskily, "I've been thinking

about us. I wanted . . . well, I wanted to know if you've been thinking about us, too. I mean . . ." Good grief. Even to her own ears she sounded like a tongue-tied teenager. This wasn't the way she had planned it.

"Jesus, honey. I think about you all the time," he said hoarsely. The buttons of her blouse slipped open beneath his fingers and he groaned softly against her throat as his hand moved down over her breast. "All the time."

"You do?" She gasped as he pushed his hand up under the lacy camisole she was wearing. His thumb found the exquisitely throbbing nipple and gently coaxed it forth. Her own fingers sank languidly into the hard muscles at the back of his neck.

"You must know by now what you do to me." He caught one of her wrists and dragged her hand down across his chest to his thigh. "Feel me, sweetheart. If you need any evidence, just touch me. All I have to do is watch you walk across a room and the next thing I know I'm in this condition."

"Oh, Zac," she breathed as his hand guided hers to the waiting hardness of him.

"I feel like I'm going to explode." He released her fingers and went back to stroking her breast with slow tantalizing movements. Gradually his hand traveled lower and with his arm around her shoulders he eased her down onto the bed. Guinevere felt the teasing thrill of excitement that flared in her lower body and knew she was rapidly nearing the point of no return. Already she was softening under his touch, yearning for the heavy weight of him, and she sensed Zac was well aware of her reaction. She had never known what it was like to literally ache for a man's possession until she had met Zac.

The urgency and immediacy of his physical effect on her was one of the things that made her wary and uncertain of the relationship. It was one of the things that had to be put aside so that a genuine dialogue could take place. Belatedly Guinevere remembered her own plans for the weekend.

"Zac?"

"We haven't got much time, honey. Here, lift up so I can get your skirt off."

"Zac, wait a minute, I think—"

"It'll be okay, sweetheart. Damn it, I didn't want to rush this." He fumbled with the zipper of her skirt.

"Zac, please, listen to me." Her fingers closed over his fumbling hand at the fastening of her skirt. "I wanted—I wanted to talk."

"We'll talk in the morning, I promise. Right now we haven't got enough time to talk and make love."

"Then we'll have to make a choice, won't we?" she said heatedly as some of her determination returned.

He agreed instantly. "Right. We'll talk later. Right now I'm going to lay you down on this bed, take off every stitch of clothing you've got on, and let you wrap yourself around me the way you do when you finally let go. God, I can't get enough of you when you come alive under me, Gwen. You're so soft and hot and clinging, and it's been so long since we've been together."

"Fourteen days," she reminded him grimly. "That's hardly a lengthy separation."

"Feels like a lifetime." He sprawled across her, locking her securely under him with his thigh. His fingers traveled up under the hem of the skirt he hadn't yet succeeded in removing and Gwen flinched passionately as he probed purposefully under her panties.

She planted her palms firmly on his shoulders, telling herself that she had to take a stand now or she would be lost beneath the tide of passion. "Zac, please. This isn't the way I had planned it. I want to talk. We *have* to talk."

He stilled above her, finally sensing her determination.

She looked up into his shadowed face and saw the gleam of his hungry gaze. For a moment Guinevere faltered before the fire in him, but the need to settle the fundamentals of the relationship was stronger tonight than even her physical need of him. Settling things was the reason she had maneuvered him into this trip, she reminded herself. She must be strong for both of them.

"You want to talk," he repeated roughly, staring down at her.

Guinevere nodded, moistening her lower lip with her tongue. "Yes. Please. It's very important."

"Obviously." Zac sighed heavily and eased himself to a sitting position. "Somehow I knew things were going to go wrong. I think I'm under a curse this weekend."

"This is serious, Zac. It's important to me." Guinevere sat up slowly, a part of her already missing the warmth of his touch. Awkwardly she began refastening the buttons of the yellow silk blouse.

"What exactly do you want to talk about?" He sounded resigned.

She gathered her courage. "I think we should discuss the status of our relationship," she said very formally.

"Oh, hell." He let his head sink into his hands.

Guinevere looked at him worriedly. "Don't you agree, Zac? I mean, we've just been sort of floundering along for several weeks now and I think it's time we put things in perspective, so to speak. I think we should assess exactly what we each want out of this association of ours and determine the boundaries. I've been feeling very confused lately, Zac. Very unsure of what's going on between us. We need to clarify matters."

"You sound as if you've been reading a lot of magazines lately."

She stiffened, hurt by the sarcasm in his voice. "I don't think I'm asking too much."

"What are you asking?"

"I just told you!"

"Well, I don't know what you mean by clarifying matters. I thought things were fairly clear a few minutes ago when we were lying down."

"I see. That's all our relationship means to you? A convenient source of sex?"

His head came up and his eyes glittered in the darkness. "Hardly what I'd call convenient. I can count on the fingers of one hand the number of times you've let me get that close. I can't figure out why you're always moving just out of range. I know by now that I can make you want me. I know I can satisfy you. What's wrong, Gwen? Why the shadow dancing? Come to think of it, I'd like a little clarification in this relationship too. I'd like to know if I'm going to have to worry about every fast-talking executive you have for a client. I'd like to know if you expect a relationship in which you can feel free to flirt with every joker who comes along in a leather flight jacket. And I'd like to know what the hell you think you're doing leading me on here on your bed and then throwing cold water on everything by announcing it's discussion time!"

Guinevere winced at that, but then she brightened. "I think this is very healthy, Zac. I think this is exactly the sort of talk we need to have." She was about to continue when her eye was caught by a shadowy movement outside the window.

"Healthy!" Zac said, outraged. "You call this *healthy?* Christ, lady, you've got a strange sense of—" He broke off, seeing her stare past him. "What's wrong?"

She gestured uncertainly. "I'm not sure. I could have sworn I just saw Vandyke walk through the gardens. He was heading toward the cliffs." Guinevere slid off the bed and went to the window.

"In that weather? It's blowing up for a storm out there."

"I know. And it's very cold. I wonder why he would be taking a walk now?" Guinevere tried to make out Vandyke's disappearing form. Zac was standing behind her, watching the man's movements as he left the garden and vanished in the direction of the cliffs.

"That sea will be really kicking up out there by now," Zac mused.

"Oh my God, Zac. What if he's had a few too many drinks and decided to do something stupid?"

"You're thinking about that gold-plated pistol you found in the executive washroom, aren't you?"

She nodded, feeling his hands close reassuringly on her shoulders. "I can't quite see Vandyke as suicidal, but there's been so much bothering him lately. Zac, if he fell into that sea in this stormy weather he might not be able to get back out in time. He'd die in that cold water, even if he could keep himself afloat."

"You mean if he jumps into that sea, don't you?"

"I've never known anyone who might be suicidal, Zac. I'm not sure of the signs. Carla went through a severe depression after her affair with Starr, but she never got to the point of threatening to kill herself."

"Vandyke hasn't threatened it either. But maybe he wouldn't. Maybe he'd just go ahead and do it, if things got bad enough." Zac released her. "I guess I'd better go bring in the sheep."

She spun around to see him pick up his jacket and head for the door. "You're going after him?"

"Why not? I haven't got anything else to do, except sit here and chat until it's time to go back to my own room."

Guinevere's mouth tightened. "There's no need for sarcasm."

"It provides a modicum of relief. God knows I could

use some relief. Good night, Gwen." He slammed the door with subdued violence as he left the room.

Zac made his way down the hall with long deliberate strides, pushing open the door at the far end to step out into the chill night. Shoving his hands into his tweed sports jacket he bent his head against the wind and wished he'd gone back to his room first to collect a real coat. It was colder than hell out here. Much warmer back in Gwen's bed, even if she was intent on having a discussion about their relationship.

On one level he was forced to admit that he agreed with her. He too had been frustrated by the ambiguities and uncertainties in their association. Zac knew he wanted to get some things ironed out and clarified. But he'd been sure it would be simpler and more straightforward to have the necessary discussion after a blissfully passionate weekend at a luxurious resort. Or to put it somewhat more bluntly, he had sensed the talk would be better conducted after a couple of nights of concentrated sex. Guinevere was always so soft and warm and amenable after he'd made love to her. Relationship discussions with her were undoubtedly safer when held while her defenses were down.

The truth was, he was not anxious to sit down and hammer out the details of their relationship with Guinevere when she was in full command of herself. It would be too much like negotiating a business arrangement. She was a strong independent woman, and when she was in top form she was formidable. Much better to reason with her after she'd been softened up a bit, Zac told himself. With a woman like Gwen a man had to resort to strategy on occasion.

He was pursuing that line of thought when he caught a shadowy movement out of the corner of his eye. There was someone else in the garden. Even as he watched, the

54

other night-walker vanished behind a hedge. Maybe someone trying to walk off a few alcoholic fumes before bedtime, Zac decided. He continued on through the gardens and into the grove of windblown firs that lined the cliffs above the sea. The moon obligingly slipped between clouds, providing some temporary illumination. In its pale gleam Zac saw Vandyke's figure hunched forlornly at the edge of the cliff.

Zac halted at the fringe of trees, aware of a deep uncertainty. He didn't know a damn thing about dealing with suicidal types. If Guinevere was right about Vandyke's state of mind, this was going to be tricky. Suddenly Zac wished Guinevere had come with him. She had an instinctive way of handling people that would make her much more useful in the present circumstances. Gritting his teeth against the cold and the task that lay before him, he started forward again.

In that same instant another figure arrived at the edge of the trees a few yards away. Zac's instincts immediately took command, instincts that had been nicely refined for survival. Obeying them was second nature to him. He leapt forward.

"Vandyke! Get down!"

The man at the edge of the cliffs turned slowly in bewilderment and found himself knocked flat on the craggy surface. He was quickly rolled behind a small heap of scruffy shrubs and boulders.

"What in hell . . . ?" Vandyke struggled to free himself.

"Hold still." Zac kept him pinned with one arm while he scanned the trees. There was no movement now. "Someone in the trees. He was watching you."

"Watching me? But I don't understand. I—Is that a gun you have?" Vandyke stared keenly at the object in Zac's hand.

"Unfortunately, no." Zac tossed aside the rock he had grabbed a few seconds earlier. "Should it be?" he asked in a level voice as he allowed Vandyke to sit up. Whoever had been there had gone now, Zac was certain of it.

Vandyke shook his head. "I don't know." He sounded vague, disoriented. Zac saw him give himself a small shake as if taking a grip on his nerve. "It's just that Guinevere said something about you going armed."

"Gwen sometimes exaggerates. She's very conscious of business images. You want to tell me what's going on, Vandyke?"

Vandyke glanced up nervously and then looked away. "Nothing's going on. I came out here to take a little stroll before going to bed. Probably whoever you saw was doing the same thing."

"Probably." Zac let the patent disbelief show in his voice. "Well, whoever it was, he's gone now. Let's get back to the hotel. A man could freeze out here."

"Yes. Yes, it's very cold, isn't it." Vandyke stumbled to his feet. "I'm sorry about this, Zac. I didn't mean to alarm you."

"Do you always go out walking in storms without bothering to put on a coat?"

Vandyke exhaled slowly. "I just had a call from my wife. It was upsetting. I wanted to think for a while. How did you know I was out here?"

"I saw you from Gwen's window. She and I were just saying good night."

"I see." Vandyke seemed embarrassed. "And the other person?" he asked Zac as they started back toward the hotel. "The one you said you saw in the trees?"

"I couldn't tell who it was. Just a shadow. You might be right, he might simply have been out taking a late night stroll too. Amazing how many people go walking on a night like this."

"But you said he was watching me?"

"That's the feeling I had. Look, Vandyke, how serious does this business get? Just how valuable are the documents in that briefcase?"

Vandyke was silent for a long moment. "They could mean a great deal of money to any of the other developers here tonight. The cost data alone would be worth a hundred thousand."

"But I'm the one with the briefcase tonight. Everyone in the lounge must have seen me leave with it. Why follow you?" Suddenly Zac felt light-headed as the facts hit him. He swore. "Oh, *shit.* Gwen's alone back in her room with the briefcase. Come on!"

Vandyke tried weakly to protest, falling into an awkward run as Zac yanked him back through the gardens. The older man was puffing heavily by the time they reached Guinevere's room.

"Gwen!" Zac pounded once on the door. It opened immediately. A wave of relief went through him as he watched her look first at him and then at Vandyke. "Gwen, are you okay? The briefcase—"

"The briefcase is fine," she assured him absently. "Mr. Vandyke, are you all right?"

"Just a little out of breath. Zac here was very anxious to get back to you."

Zac was in no mood for more conversation. "Hand me the briefcase, Gwen. Vandyke and I are going back to our rooms. We'll see you at breakfast."

Guinevere eyed him thoughtfully. Without a word she turned around, went and got the briefcase, and brought it back to Zac at the door.

"Good night, Gwen," he said as she handed it to him.

"Good night, Zac."

"Swell evening, huh?" he couldn't resist drawling in ill-concealed disgust.

"You really know how to show a girl a good time."

He couldn't think of an adequate response to that, so he closed the door very politely in her face and started down the hall with Vandyke, carrying the briefcase.

Chapter Four

If there had been any polite way of refusing the boat tour that was announced at breakfast on Sunday morning, Guinevere would have done so. But after a jovial Sheldon Washburn dropped by Vandyke's table to inform him he'd arranged a special excursion—by boat instead of plane, because he'd heard Miss Jones didn't care for small planes—Guinevere's social options were narrowed. Vandyke had cordially accepted on her behalf.

"Very thoughtful of you, Sheldon. I'm sure my secretary will enjoy herself. I'm afraid I'm going to need Zac here though. Who else is going along?"

"Toby Springer and two or three others who aren't needed at this morning's session." Washburn beamed at Guinevere, who tried to look properly grateful. "Miss Jones will be the only lady on the boat, but that shouldn't be too hard to take, eh, Miss Jones?"

Guinevere sighed. "I'll manage."

Washburn slapped Vandyke on the shoulder and went on to inform the others of their good fortune. Vandyke glanced uneasily at Zac, who had stoically continued to eat grapefruit during Washburn's announcement.

"You don't mind remaining here for this morning's session, Zac?"

"I'm sure Miss Jones will be able to handle a boatload

of administrative assistants, won't you, Miss Jones?" Zac gave her a bland smile.

Guinevere refused to rise to the bait. "I'm certain it will be a lovely tour. And we're in luck. We've even got a bit of sunshine."

"Yes indeed," Zac agreed. "Luck is just overflowing around here today. Can't remember when I've felt so lucky."

Guinevere waited until after breakfast to corner him. She pinned him down in the rustic lobby, where he was patiently waiting for Vandyke. The briefcase was at his side.

"What happened last night, Zac?" Guinevere dropped down onto the sofa beside him, her brows in a straight demanding line.

"I got cold. In more ways than one."

"I'm serious. What went on out there on the cliff?" she hissed. "Was he really trying to kill himself?"

Zac sighed. "Beats the hell out of me. I can't read minds. But someone else was out there watching the whole scene."

"Someone else was outside in that storm?"

"Yeah. I guess I overreacted. I didn't know what was going on, so I tackled Vandyke and dragged him behind some cover. You'd have been proud of me, Gwen. I really did a nice job of reinforcing the old commando image. At least, until my client realized all I had in my hand was a rock, not a gun. But whoever had followed him didn't hang around. Very anticlimactic."

Guinevere examined his jacket intently. "Where is your gun?"

"Back home in Seattle."

She was shocked. "You didn't bring it with you?"

"I was under the impression that all I had to do this weekend was keep sticky fingers out of a briefcase. I had a couple of other items on my agenda, too, but none of them required a weapon." He sounded aggrieved.

Guinevere bit her lip, torn between sympathy and amusement. Impulsively she put a hand on his sleeve. "You can't come with us on this harbor jaunt?"

He looked at her. "You heard Vandyke. Not that it makes much difference. Everything else about this weekend is getting fouled up, so I might as well earn my pay. You're right about your client, Gwen. He's scared to death. I think he'll feel a lot better if I stay close to him. And since I've decided to actually work this weekend, I think I'll make a couple of phone calls."

"To whom? About what?"

"I love it when you get excited. The only problem is, you're picking the wrong time and place."

"Zac! Quit baiting me. Tell me who you're going to call."

"Someone who used to work for my old firm. He had the Caribbean region during the seventies. He quit the company in nineteen eighty to devote his life to rum and writing the great American novel, but he stayed in Saint Thomas. I thought I'd see if he can dig up some info on the accident."

"What accident?" Guinevere asked, momentarily lost. "Oh! You mean the plane accident that killed Vandyke's partner."

"It's not normal to carry around a page out of a dead man's logbook, Gwen."

"You can say that again. It's downright morbid." Guinevere gave the matter some thought. "Maybe I can weasel out of this scenic tour."

"Forget it." Zac glanced over her shoulder at Vandyke, approaching across the lobby. "It will take Sol a while to dig up any real information. That's assuming I can get hold of him in the first place." He got to his feet. "Have fun," he whispered into her ear, quickly brushing her nose with a kiss. "Sorry about that. I know it's bad for the image, but I couldn't resist." He was gone before Guinevere could tell him wistfully that she didn't really mind the small kiss in public.

Two hours later she found herself in the back of the fair-size cabin cruiser Sheldon Washburn had hired for the occasion. Three of the other assistants had also been freed by their employers to take the trip. The surprise passenger was Cassidy. When he'd stepped onto the boat, grinning at her with charming wickedness, Guinevere had experienced a small twinge of guilt. Utterly ridiculous, of course, she told herself. She was certainly not to blame if Cassidy blithely chose to crash the cruise party. There was no way on earth Zac could take her to task for it. Besides, she didn't owe Zac undying fealty. They hadn't even had the big relationship discussion yet. And she was hardly contemplating anything resembling betrayal in any case! The whole situation was simply, clearly, undeniably not her fault. But she was secretly glad Zac didn't know who had joined the small group on the scenic tour. Some things were better left unmentioned.

Cassidy's grin grew decidedly broader as he chose the seat next to hers. He stayed there during the entire trip, one booted foot braced against the seat in front of him, his left arm casually draped across the back of Guinevere's chair. In a laid-back laconic manner he supplemented the travelogue the boat's pilot was giving.

"Have you flown to most of these little islands?" Guinevere asked politely at one point. In the rare morning sunlight the gems of lush green seemed to have been sprinkled in the water by a careless hand.

"No point flying to some of them," Cassidy told her. "No one lives on them. And some you couldn't beach the

Cessna on anyway. They're just tree-covered rocks, without any natural coves or bays."

"I've heard some of them are privately owned."

Toby Springer caught the comment and remarked, "Washburn is thinking about buying one." There was a touch of pride in his voice. Springer clearly admired his boss's success.

"Really?" Guinevere asked, interested. "Near here?"

"Over there, I think. Isn't that the one, Cassidy? You took him there once in your plane."

Cassidy nodded, showing a supreme lack of interest. "Yeah."

"Does he have a home on it?" Guinevere peered at the small, thickly forested island.

"He's considering building one, but he hasn't gotten around to it," Springer told her. "No one lives there right now. It would be strictly an investment."

One of the other men who had been freed for the day joined the conversation. He was a young intense man with round preppy glasses and a thin face. His name was Milton Tanner. "Your boss has done pretty well on his investments. He'll probably find a way to turn that one into a fortune too."

Springer nodded. "Washburn's done okay."

Milt Tanner's face relaxed in a brief smile. "You can say that again. I got the job of researching him for my boss before we decided to make the proposal for the resort. He seems to have come out of nowhere in the mid seventies and has managed to keep a low profile, but there's a lot of money behind him."

"He's smart and he knows land values." Springer grinned. "Why do you think I work for him? He's tough, but I wanted to learn from the best."

"How long have you been with him?" Guinevere asked, aware that Cassidy was growing restless beside

63

her. He didn't appreciate the conversation having taken a turn that more or less left him out of it.

"A year," Springer said. "Another cup of coffee?"

"Sounds great." Guinevere smiled. "There may be sun out here today but it's downright chilly."

"I can take care of that little problem," Cassidy drawled, blue eyes glinting with meaning.

"Uh-uh." Guinevere smiled. "I think I'm safer with the coffee."

"People who always want to be safe miss a lot in life, Guinevere Jones. You don't really live unless you take a few chances." Cassidy's voice was soft, pitched for her ears alone. "It would be a shame if a woman like you missed too much along the way. I get the feeling you were born to take a few risks."

Guinevere tilted her head to one side, considering that. "I think you've made a slight miscalculation, Cassidy. The only risks I was born to take are those involved in running a small business, and I have to take more than enough of those."

He shook his head, eyes narrowed against the watery sunlight. "Trust me, honey. I could make you change your mind."

Guinevere smiled. He really was amusing. That kind of man often was. But a wise woman didn't expect anything more than superficial entertainment from such a man. It was all they were capable of providing. If you looked for anything else you were doomed to disappointment. There was something missing, something a perceptive woman couldn't always put her finger on but that she sensed was lacking. Guinevere knew that if she went looking for a complete man beneath Cassidy's flashy exterior she wouldn't find one.

The breeze seemed to turn colder as the boat headed back toward the marina.

The weather, however, was not nearly as cold as the expression in Zac's gray eyes as he stood on the dock an hour later waiting for the returning boat to be made fast. Guinevere hadn't noticed him until the last minute, and when she did she groaned inwardly. So much for small discretions. Cassidy was standing behind her, big as life, and she sensed his amused satisfaction as he solicitously helped her ashore.

"Anytime you want a private tour you just let me know, Gwen," he murmured as Zac came forward. "I can always squeeze you into my schedule. And you can see a hell of a lot more from the air."

"Thank you," she said lamely, aware of Zac's bleak expression. She turned to him with a deliberately cheerful smile. "Oh, hello, Zac. I didn't know you'd be able to meet me. Did the conference get out early?"

"No."

"I see. Well, we had a great tour of the area."

"I can imagine. You ready to go back to the hotel? It's almost time for lunch."

He wasn't going to be gracious or understanding about this, apparently. A small flame of resentment started to uncurl within her. Damn it anyway, she told herself. Who was Zac Justis to make her feel guilty over a social situation that had been totally beyond her control? She didn't like the feeling and she didn't like the fact that Zac could induce it. This relationship she was involved in had to be clarified, and soon. She knew she was glowering as Zac opened the Buick's door and unceremoniously all but shoved her inside. The others were driving back to the resort in Springer's car.

"It wasn't my fault, you know," she muttered, and immediately resented the fact that she'd felt obliged to defend herself. "Cassidy just showed up at the last minute and hopped aboard."

"How fitting. Hopalong Cassidy."

"It's not nice to make fun of a person's disability."

"Did he regale you with the tale of how he managed to collect such a romantic limp? I'll bet it's a great story, full of heroism and danger." Zac grimly turned the key in the ignition.

"No, he did not. As a matter of fact we discussed the local islands, and then some of us talked a bit about Washburn's success. He's thinking of buying one of those empty islands out there, you know."

"No, I didn't know. But I'm not surprised. What's that got to do with anything?"

"Well, nothing. I just thought you were asking for a blow-by-blow account of the cruise, so I was trying to give it to you."

"Spare me. If I want the account, I'll ask for it."

"Yes, sir. You certainly are in a good mood, sir, if I may say so, sir. Did anything interesting happen between Washburn and Vandyke at the conference?"

Zac's mouth hardened. "I think Vandyke's going to get the deal."

Guinevere glanced at him. "Really? That's great. Maybe that will make him relax a little."

"It's not final yet, and Vandyke doesn't seem any more relaxed." Zac turned the corner onto the narrow road that led from the small village back to the resort.

Guinevere sought for more neutral conversation. "Did you get hold of your friend?"

"Sol? Yeah. He was sleeping off a hangover. Said he'd look into it when I told him I'd send along a check to cover his expenses. His great American novel hasn't yet found a publisher, I gather."

"So we don't know any more than we did this morning?"

"Nope."

"Where's the briefcase?"

"Vandyke has it. I think he felt guilty about asking me to stick so close when that wasn't really what he'd hired me to do. He told me to take off for a few minutes to collect you. We're meeting him for lunch."

Wonderful, Guinevere thought morosely. Zac was right. The weekend wasn't working out at all. At least not the way she'd hoped it would. She propped her elbow on the padded door and leaned her chin on her hand, gazing out the window at the tree-lined road.

"Zac?"

"Yeah?"

"Are you really upset about Cassidy being along on that cruise?"

There was a beat of heavy silence. "I shouldn't be, should I?" he asked grimly.

She slid him a sidelong glance. "No. You shouldn't. For one thing, I had nothing to do with it. And for another, we haven't . . ." She faltered.

"We haven't had that little chat you want, have we?" he finished for her.

"Well, no."

"Is this chat of ours going to include some kind of agreement regarding outside relationships? Is that the right expression?"

She drew a deep breath, concentrating fiercely on the narrow winding road. "I had thought it might."

There was another heavy silence. Then Zac said slowly, obviously choosing his words with care, "Gwen, I am not normally a possessive man."

That surprised her. "You aren't?"

"It's worked reasonably well over the years, since women do not tend to get possessive about me."

"I see." She felt an immediate surge of sheer undiluted feminine possessiveness. The thought of Zac taking someone else out to dinner and discussing such things as a business image and IRS deductions for small firms was enough to make her stomach tighten, she realized suddenly. Until now she had only considered the situation from her side. She had been wary of what she had thought was his growing demand for exclusivity. Now she was forced to take a hard look at her own feelings for him.

"It's different with you, Gwen," he finally said. He sounded very grim about it.

She turned her head. "It is?"

He kept his eyes on the road. "I think so."

"You only think so?" She felt incipient panic.

He exhaled slowly and said very steadily, "Gwen, it's hard enough not knowing what you're doing or who you're with on the nights when you're not with me. If I thought you were sleeping with someone else— It would rip me apart."

She caught her breath at the stark honesty of the statement. "Oh, Zac. I didn't realize . . . I didn't know . . ."

He ignored her. "I know you're used to being free, totally independent. So am I, for that matter. But with me it was kind of a moot point. My social life isn't exactly hectic."

"Neither is mine," she said quietly. He had been honest with her. She decided it was time to take the same step herself. "Zac, I'm not seeing anyone else. I haven't dated anyone else since I met you."

He did glance at her then, gray eyes full of urgency. "No one?"

"No one."

He chewed on that for a moment. "For what it's worth, neither have I," he said.

"Zac?"

68

"Yeah?"

"It's worth a lot."

There was a great deal of silence for the remainder of the short drive, but it wasn't an unpleasant silence. Guinevere was aware of the tentative commitment that had just been made between herself and Zac. It wasn't exactly a formal declaration of the status of their relationship, she decided, but it was a step in the right direction. It was also a little scary, for reasons she didn't want to consider.

Vandyke was waiting impatiently for them when they returned. He seemed relieved to see Zac. He also had work for Guinevere. She spent the afternoon typing up some modifications to one of the proposals, which effectively destroyed any possibility of more time with Zac.

By dinner she was resigned to the inevitability of the failure of the weekend from a personal point of view. It was obvious that Zac had reached the same decision and had decided to give the client what he wanted. He kept unobtrusively within sight of Vandyke most of the time and after dinner he followed his client into the lounge. Guinevere accompanied them, but by eleven o'clock she decided there was no point stretching out the evening any longer.

She politely said her good nights, smiling tentatively at Zac. He gave her a long level look and shrugged fatalistically. She knew he was going to stay in his own room that night. What really bothered her was that he didn't show any signs of inviting her to stay with him. She must have really frozen him out last night with her insistence on a dialogue.

"Think I'll turn in too," Vandyke announced, rising with Guinevere. "What about you, Justis?"

"Doesn't seem to be much in the way of alternatives. One thing about these resorts in the winter—they're restful."

Guinevere saw Vandyke's brief expression of commiseration but the older man made no move to excuse Zac from guard duty. Twenty minutes later Guinevere was alone in her room, wondering where she'd gone wrong when she'd first schemed to drag Zac along on the trip to the San Juans. She sat down on the edge of the bed to take off her pantyhose.

"Ah, well, the best laid plans—oh, damn," she finished, reacting to the bad snag her fingernails had just made in the upper left leg of the pantyhose. "Zac's right. Nothing is going properly this weekend." She marched over to the wastebasket beside the dresser to drop them into it, but reconsidered. The snag was high on the leg. She wouldn't risk wearing the pantyhose under a skirt but she could get away with wearing them under slacks. Guinevere wadded them up and went to put them in the left-hand side of her suitcase. The good pantyhose were in little bundles on the right-hand side, and she didn't want to get them mixed up. In the morning she wasn't always perfectly alert to such details as snags.

That high-level decision made, Guinevere puttered around the room a while longer, changing into her long-sleeved cotton nightgown, brushing her teeth, and generally killing time preparing for bed. Then, very much aware of the empty bed, she picked up a paperback and tried reading for a while. But her thoughts kept straying to the cautious discussion she'd had with Zac in the car. Outside another high wind announced that a new storm was on its way. So much for the brief sunshine the San Juans had enjoyed that morning.

By midnight Guinevere gave up trying to read. She put the book down beside the bed and slid out from under the covers. Switching off the light, she went to the window and opened the drapes to stare out into the darkness of the incoming storm, leaning against the window frame and contemplating the new era of relationships between men and women.

Life was definitely not simpler in the modern age.

Why hadn't Zac made some attempt to convince her to come to his room tonight, if it was true he felt obliged to stay there because of Vandyke? Perhaps he felt rebuffed after last night. Guinevere winced. She hadn't handled last night very well. It was understandable if Zac felt she had been holding him at bay—in a sense she had been doing exactly that. And she wasn't sure she could explain quite why, even to herself.

Restlessly Guinevere moved around the room, picking up objects off the dresser, fiddling with the thermostat, listening to the gathering wind. It was when she found herself trying to reread the same page of the paperback that she finally came to a decision. This was a new era, she lectured herself. Zac hadn't invited her to his room, but nothing said she couldn't invite herself.

With a sudden sense of determination she yanked off the nightgown and stepped into her jeans without bothering to put on any underwear. She skipped a bra, too, when she reached for her wide-sleeved, oversize poet's shirt. She wouldn't bother with shoes. No one was likely to see her in the hall and even if someone did, the ballet-style slippers she was wearing were fine. Taking a grip on her resolve, Guinevere opened the door to her room, glanced both ways, and started down the empty corridor to Zac's room.

He was right. It did seem a very long way, especially at this hour of the night. She heard voices in a few of the rooms as she passed the doors, but she saw no one. When she reached Zac's door she raised her hand to knock. Suddenly she was overcome by a thousand second thoughts.

71

The door opened before she could commit her knuckles to the knock.

"I thought I heard someone out here," Zac muttered in a low growl. "What the hell are you doing here?"

He was wearing a pair of slacks and nothing else. Guinevere swallowed a little uncertainly. She looked up at him, appealing for understanding. "I came to say good night. No, that's not quite right. I came to spend the night."

He stared down at her. "The hell you did. Guinevere Jones, how can you do this to me? I'm going to spend the rest of the night in agony."

That shook her. "Agony?" Her eyes widened unhappily.

"Because you can't stay, you little idiot. I've told you, there's a connecting door between my room and Vandyke's. It's nothing more than a thin sheet of plywood, for crying out loud. Now get your sweet tail back down that hall before I lose my perspective on your business image."

Guinevere touched his bare shoulder with her fingertips. "I'll be very quiet, Zac. I promise."

He closed his eyes briefly in despair. When he opened them again there was a new element swirling in the gray depths. Guinevere knew that element. She'd seen it before. It sent a tremor of excitement through her. It also gave her courage.

"I want to stay, Zac."

"Honey, I'd give my right arm to have you stay. But for your own sake—"

"I'll worry about my own image." She smiled gently and went past him into the room, turning to watch as he slowly closed the door behind her. When he met her eyes she knew he had lost his small inner battle. Without a word he held out his arms, and she went into them just as silently.

"Zac, I'm sorry about last night," she said after a while.

"Hush, honey. Please hush." He stroked her head, his body strong and urgent against hers. Then he buried his lips in her loose, slightly tangled brown hair and inhaled deeply. "Christ, I want you. I want you so damn much. . . ."

She clung to him, her fingertips digging into the sleek skin of his broad shoulders as he unfastened her jeans.

"You forgot something," he murmured, discovering she wasn't wearing any panties.

"I dressed in a hurry," she admitted in a tiny whisper.

"I'm glad."

His palms cupped her full hips as she stepped out of the jeans. Luxuriously he gripped her, lifting her against the warmth of his lower body. His mouth moved urgently on hers and Gwen parted her lips to allow his tongue to enter deep inside. She could feel him hard and aroused against her and it sparked the excitement in her veins. Her arms wound around his neck.

She felt herself lifted off her toes and carried to the turned back bed. Zac settled her in the middle and straightened to unzip his slacks. His eyes never left her as she lay there waiting for him, and when he finally stood naked before her she could already feel the beginnings of the delicious tension he created. He switched off the light and lay down on the bed. She felt his heavy thigh move across her languidly twisting leg, the hairy roughness of it making her moan softly.

"Shush," he muttered and covered her mouth with his own.

She ignored him, sighing into his mouth. How could she worry about the thinness of a connecting door when her whole body was starting to clamor for the satisfaction it knew it could get only from this one particular man? He drank the small sound she made, his hand stroking down over her breast. She could feel the faint trembling of anticipation in his fingers and gloried in the knowledge that he was barely able to hold himself in check. Being wanted this badly by Zachariah Justis was a powerful aphrodisiac, one she knew she was becoming addicted to. Her body lifted against his probing touch, seeking the vital masculinity of him. He pressed against her hip and she could feel the eagerness in him.

"Ah, Gwen, my sweet, soft Gwen." The words were as thick and sweet as honey as Zac reluctantly tore his mouth from hers and began to nibble hungrily elsewhere.

She clenched her fingers in his hair as his lips and tongue forged a sizzling path down to the peaks of her breasts, hovering there for a moment until she caught her breath and tried to urge him closer. Then he was moving lower.

His body was an enthralling seductive weight on her own as he sprawled over her. She felt the damp heat of his mouth in the small dip of her stomach, and then he was using his teeth with exciting gentleness on the inside of her thigh. He held her legs apart with his big hands and began a slow tantalizing trail of kisses back up to the part of her that was already damp with desire.

Guinevere moaned, turning her head into the pillow. Her knees flexed upward as the tension within her grew to overpowering proportions.

"Zac . . . Please, Zac. I want you so."

Slowly he made his way back up the length of her. He was hard and taut with his own need, and in the shadowy light she could see the fierce hunger in his eyes. His face was tight with the force of the urgency driving him. He lowered himself deliberately down onto her, holding her knees in their raised position. He teased her, probing slighty and then withdrawing, until Guinevere thought she would go out of her mind.

"Zac!" Heedless of anything but the need to have him fill her completely, Guinevere clutched at his back. "I can't wait any longer," she whispered into his neck.

"Neither can I." He surged against her, driving deep into her tight silken core.

Guinevere cried out, but he must have been expecting the husky sound because he once more sealed her mouth with his own. The soft feminine sob of excitement was lost in his throat. She could feel the groan of desire that rippled through his chest in response.

Quickly he established the primitive rhythm, drawing her with him down the spiraling trail. She wrapped her legs around him, abandoning herself to the thrilling ride and feeling the tightening of his muscles as he forged toward his own satisfaction. Guinevere was lost in the sensual whirlpool. The universe narrowed until it was filled only with Zac and the night. When the tension within her finally burst free of its bonds she cried out again.

Zac held her shivering body, trying to trap the delightful sounds of her climax even as he gave way to his own. In the end he knew he could not have successfully concealed Guinevere's presence in his room from the man next door.

The only thing that saved them both was the ringing of Vandyke's telephone just as Guinevere went over the edge. Zac hoped the noise had masked the final sounds of satisfaction. It was odd, he reflected vaguely as the phone next door was answered. He collapsed in a damp sprawl on Guinevere's equally damp body. On the one hand he wanted to shout to the world that this woman was his. On the other he felt a fierce desire to protect her. He knew how carefully she maintained her business image. He hadn't wanted to jeopardize it for her. But there was no way on earth he could have held out against her tonight.

At first Guinevere didn't know if the phone was ringing on the table next to Zac's bed or in Vandyke's room. By the time she surfaced far enough to figure it out, she could hear Vandyke's soft muffled voice.

"Cathy," Vandyke muttered.

Guinevere's eyes opened as she heard the name. "His wife," she whispered to Zac.

Zac shook himself a little, apparently trying to clear his head. He lifted himself away from Guinevere. "Good. That will keep him occupied. He won't hear you leaving."

"But Zac, I don't want to leave."

"Move, woman. I should never have let you stay. Get dressed and get out of here." He gave her a small push and then pulled her back for a quick hard kiss before shoving her to the edge of the bed.

Resentfully, Guinevere did as she was told. A part of her recognized that it would be best if she exited from her own room in the morning. People talked, and while the times had indeed become more liberal, people still loved to talk most about the affairs of others. Small businesspersons did not need too much of that kind of gossip.

Fumbling, she got back into her pants and shirt. Zac opened the door for her and she darted a quick glance down the hall. It was empty.

"Go," he hissed softly, but his eyes were gleaming with remembered passion.

She went, making it back to her own room without incident and falling into bed, convinced she wouldn't be able to sleep. She slept like a log. It wasn't until she was putting on her pantyhose the next morning that she realized someone had searched her room while she had been with Zac.

Chapter Five

He didn't feel like a frog the next morning, Zac reflected in lazy contentment. But then, he never did after a night that included Guinevere Jones in his bed. He yawned hugely, pushing back the blankets, and went into the bathroom. Guinevere had called him a frog the first time they had met. Of course, he reminded himself tolerantly, she'd had reason to view him in a somewhat negative light. He'd been blackmailing her at the time.

Zac leaned into the shower and turned on the water full blast. While he waited for the water to get hot he stretched, aware of the pleasant aftereffects of Guinevere's sweet passion. He always felt good the next morning. Strong, healthy, brilliant—and sexy as hell.

She had a way of making him feel this good. Zac didn't fully understand it and saw absolutely no need to try. It was a fact. A smart man made a grab for the good things in life and didn't waste time questioning them or tearing them apart to examine them analytically.

Guinevere, on the other hand, seemed to want to talk lately. Zac stepped into the shower, wondering if yesterday's conversation in the car on the way back from the marina had been sufficient for her. He'd gotten what he needed out of the chat. He grinned a little to himself as he applied soap to his chest. She wasn't seeing anyone else. She hadn't seen anyone else since she'd met him.

Zac realized his idiotic grin was widening. He shoved his head under the spray.

She was late coming down to breakfast that morning. Zac joined a subdued Vandyke for coffee and a platter of bacon and eggs. Guinevere still hadn't appeared by the time Washburn took Vandyke and the other two business executives into a conference room for what was to be the last round of presentations. Vandyke hesitated before following the others, glancing worriedly down at Zac, who was still drinking coffee.

"You're going to stick around in case I, uh, need you later, right, Justis?"

"I'll be here. Good luck with the presentation."

Vandyke nodded brusquely and turned to go. Zac watched him leave, feeling helpless to reassure the man. He understood now why Guinevere was worried about her client. Vandyke was a man walking the razor's edge.

The conference room door closed behind the high-level executives just as Guinevere entered the coffee shop. Zac watched her scan the small crowd, which consisted of Toby Springer and the handful of other people who had accompanied their bosses to the resort. He waited with a sense of pleasant anticipation for the moment she spotted him sitting by the window.

She managed to look both chic and casual against the gloom of another rainy morning. The sweater she was wearing was a rich bronze color trimmed in black, and the pleated black pants had a wide band that emphasized her small waist and the full flare of her hips. Zac remembered the feel of her in the night and exhaled slowly.

She had wanted him badly enough last night to risk her image. That realization threatened to go to his head like hot brandy. The idea of Guinevere Jones sneaking down a hotel hallway just to be with him was enough to get him aroused all over again. He drew in another breath and again let it out with slow control. Sophisticated business security consultants did not allow their bodies to embarrass them in public restaurants. At that moment Guinevere turned and caught him watching her. She started toward him purposefully.

"I need to talk to you," she announced in a low tone as she sat down across from him. Her hazel eyes were narrowed and steady. The mouth that had been so soft and warm during the night was firm with resolve.

Zac groaned. "I was afraid of that."

Her brows came together in that funny way they did when she was about to deliver a lecture. "Zac, this is serious."

"I can tell."

Guinevere's frown deepened as she realized he wasn't ready to show the proper concern. What was the matter with him this morning? She leaned forward intently. "Zac, somebody searched my room last night."

He stared at her.

"Well, at least I've got your attention." She sat back, satisfied.

"Searched your room?" He looked dumbfounded.

She nodded with grave certainty. "Must have happened while I was . . ." She glanced away. "With you," she finished, looking at him again.

"You were only with me about half an hour." He ignored her flicker of embarrassment. "Gwen, are you sure? Why didn't you come and get me? How do you know you were searched? Were things messed up?"

"Oh, no. It was a very professional job."

"No offense, but how would you know if your room had been professionally tossed?"

She wrinkled her nose. "Tossed?"

"Forget it." He glanced up as the waitress approached and waited impatiently while the woman poured coffee and Guinevere ordered cereal and fruit. Then he folded his arms in front of him on the table. "Tell me what happened," he said deliberately.

Guinevere sighed inwardly. She had known it would be like this, of course. Zac would want a blow-by-blow account, complete in every detail. He was a careful thorough man who tended to take his time about this sort of thing. He himself admitted that he worked slow. When he'd worked for the international group of private security consultants, she knew, his co-workers had nicknamed him "the Glacier"—slow-moving, but in the end everything got covered.

"I just realized what had happened this morning when I put on my pantyhose."

He blinked slowly. "Pantyhose?"

"I'm wearing a pair under these pants. They provide some extra warmth," she told him impatiently.

"I see."

"No, you don't. The first pair I put on had a run in them. On the left leg, above the knee."

"Tacky."

"Zac, you're not paying attention."

"I'm paying attention, I'm just not following the gist of this conversation. Tell me, in one-syllable words, the significance of your pantyhose having a run in them."

She made a small exclamation of disgust. "Zac, last night when I was getting ready for bed I snagged a pair of pantyhose."

"Okay, I can follow that. Go on."

"Don't be condescending. This is crucial evidence."

"I'm listening," he told her gravely.

"I didn't want them to get mixed up with my clean *un*snagged pantyhose and I didn't feel like taking the time to wash them out. So I put them in my suitcase on the left-hand side. The clean unsnagged ones are on the right. Got it so far?"

"Clear as crystal."

"Good. Well, this morning I reached for a pair from the clean side of the suitcase."

"The right side?"

"Precisely." She looked at him with faint approval. "And I got the pair I had put in on the left side last night. Whoever went through my suitcase didn't realize I'd know the difference, I suppose. Or else he was in a hurry." She waited with a gleam of triumph in her eyes.

Zac continued to gaze at her with level speculation. He was silent for a long moment. Finally, he said, "You're basing all this on one snagged pair of pantyhose? Nothing else appeared to have been touched?"

"No, it was a very careful job."

"Gwen," he said patiently, "why would anyone search your room? I'm the one who has the briefcase at night. Vandyke's the one who might have important papers to hide. You're, pardon the expression, just a secretary, as far as anyone around here is concerned."

"I don't know why someone would do it, Zac. You're the authority on business security, you tell me. Secretaries often have important notes and papers lying around. Maybe somebody was looking for something I might have left out after doing that typing for Vandyke yesterday afternoon."

"Gwen, if they went into your room during the short period you were with me, that means someone was keeping a close eye on your activities."

She shuddered. "Spooky, isn't it?"

"Also unlikely. Honey, I don't mean to let the air out of your balloon, but there's no logical reason why someone would search your room instead of mine or Vandyke's."

"How do you know they haven't searched yours?" she demanded.

He shrugged, picking up his coffee cup. "I'd know."

She saw the certainty in his face and concluded he probably would. "What about Vandyke? He's acting so strange lately I'm not sure he'd notice if anyone had been through his things."

"Or tell us if he did notice," Zac finished. "You're right there, but somehow I don't think it's happened."

"Then why me?"

"I'm not sure you were searched. One little pair of snagged pantyhose found on the wrong side of the suitcase is kind of slim evidence, Gwen. It would have been easy for you to forget which side you tossed them into. After all, when you were undressing last night you must have had your mind on . . ." He paused deliberately, and a slow satisfied smile lit his eyes. "Other things."

"Egotist."

He paid no attention. "Did you see anyone in the hall on the way back to your room last night?"

"No," she admitted, "but that doesn't mean anything. Someone could have come and gone before I left your room. Or he could have entered my room through the balcony."

"Eat your breakfast and we'll go have a look."

"You're just trying to placate me, aren't you?"

"No, I'm just trying to make sure one way or the other."

But they could find nothing else to verify Guinevere's suspicions. Zac went through the room carefully without finding anything to support the idea that someone had searched it. He shook his head and put his arm around Guinevere's shoulders. "Honey, I think it was your imagination at work. There's just no logic to it."

By now Guinevere was beginning to doubt her own

discovery of the pantyhose. She sorted through the remaining pairs. "I don't know, Zac. I could have sworn the pair I put on first this morning was the pair I had deliberately put into the left side of the suitcase. Now you've got me wondering."

He ran a fingertip down her nose. "I told you, last night you had other things on your mind." His eyes gleamed for a moment with the memories, and she tried to glare at him.

"I knew I was never going to hear the end of it." She moved away from him. "What's the schedule for today?"

"I promised Vandyke I'd stick around the lobby in case he needs me. I just wish to hell I knew what he thought he might need me for. He's got the briefcase in the conference room. This is the last round of presentations, and Washburn's promised a decision by this afternoon. We'll all get to go home early this evening. Frankly, I can't wait."

"Did Vandyke look nervous?" she asked.

"No more so than usual."

"How long did the conversation with his wife last?"

"Not long. About ten minutes after you left."

Guinevere eyed Zac thoughtfully. "I don't suppose you could actually hear what he said to her?"

He smiled. "What a little snoop. No, I couldn't catch most of the words. Just her name occasionally. The connecting door isn't that thin—thank God. It means he might not have heard you. At least, he didn't make any reference to you being in my room last night."

Guinevere considered that. "I'm not sure he would. He's really quite a gentleman."

Zac paced to the window, running a hand through his hair. "Well, one way or another this whole thing should be over this afternoon. We'll catch the ferry back to Seattle and that will be the end of my commitment to Vandyke. What about you? How long are you supposed to cover for his secretary?"

"She'll probably be back on the job tomorrow."

"Good. I can't say this little jaunt hasn't been interesting in some ways, but I'll be glad when it's over. What are you going to do today?"

"I have some typing to take care of for Vandyke this morning. Then I guess I'll pack and get ready to leave."

Zac glanced back at her as he stood in front of the window. His eyes were the same color as the overcast sky. "Do you think we might try this again sometime?"

"A wild weekend fling?"

"Yeah."

Under his deliberate gaze she felt the warmth rising in her cheeks. "That might be nice."

"Next time we won't try to combine business with pleasure. It's too damn frustrating."

Guinevere hesitated. There were other things that were frustrating. "We still haven't had a chance to really discuss things between us, Zac."

He went to her, gripped her shoulders fiercely, and planted a hard kiss on her mouth. "Personally, I thought we'd made terrific strides."

"Do you really think so?"

The phone rang just as Guinevere was waiting in an agony of hope for her answer. With a disgusted sigh she went to answer it. She listened to Vandyke's hurried instructions and hung up with a regretful sigh.

"That was Vandyke. He wants me to hurry up with that typing. Guess I'd better get busy doing what I'm being paid to do. I'll see you at lunch, Zac."

"And I'll go do my duty in the lobby," he groaned as he stalked to the door.

Guinevere watched the closed door for a long moment before she went to the typewriter that had been set up in her room. So much for all her plans to define the relationship.

Washburn's announcement shortly before lunch caught both Zac and Guinevere completely by surprise. From their client's general attitude of depression and uncertainty, they would never have guessed Vandyke Development had been selected to do the Washburn project.

"Congratulations," Guinevere said sincerely over lunch. "It's a wonderful deal. You must be quite pleased."

Vandyke nodded, but he didn't look particularly thrilled. "It's definitely a load off my mind."

If that's the case, Guinevere thought, he certainly doesn't *look* very relieved.

"I'm glad it worked out," Zac said politely, watching the older man carefully. "The announcement came sooner than expected. When do you want to leave for Seattle?"

Vandyke looked at him questioningly, seeming suddenly to realize something. "Oh, I forgot. Washburn wants us to stay over one more day to finalize things. The others are going back this afternoon, but I guess I simply assumed you and Miss Jones would be available for one more day." He glanced worriedly at Guinevere. "Can you manage? I'm going to need you to handle the final letter of agreement. Washburn and I will rough it out this afternoon."

"We had planned on getting back today," Zac began firmly, but Guinevere cut him off.

"I can manage one more day," she assured her client. "What about you, Zac?"

He glanced at her, sighing. "Yeah, I guess I can squeeze in one more day."

"I'm very grateful to both of you. Why don't you take off after lunch and do some shopping or something, Miss

Jones? I'm not going to need you until this evening, actually. It will take Washburn and myself several hours to hammer out the details. He wants to get everything wound up by tomorrow so he can get back to his offices in California. Zac, I'd appreciate it if you could hang around here?"

"Sure," Zac murmured. "Why not? Nothing I like to do better on a wild weekend."

"Zac!" Guinevere hissed warningly. Fortunately Vandyke didn't appear to have heard. He nodded vaguely, apparently satisfied, and excused himself. "I'll stay here with you," she went on to Zac, who immediately made a negative motion with his chin.

"Forget it. I'm not going to be good company and you'll enjoy hitting those little shops in town. Take your time. I'll just read a good book or something."

"What good book?"

"How about *A Thousand and One Erotic Fantasies of the Small Businessman?*"

Guinevere grinned. "Is it a best-seller?"

"It probably will be after I write it."

It was drizzling rain by three o'clock that afternoon when Guinevere finally decided she was not going to find the perfect pottery vase or an undiscovered painter in the town shops. She treated herself to a cup of hot tea and a scone at a small café and stared out the window at the rain-slick street. A few other tourists who favored the San Juans in winter were scurrying from one shop to the next, trying to avoid the gentle rain. A few cars made their way down the street with windshield wipers swishing languidly.

Guinevere thought of Zac, whom she had left sitting in the hotel lobby with a magazine, and decided she'd rather be sitting beside him. True, his good mood of the morning had disintegrated when he'd discovered they were going to have to stay another night, but she'd rather be with him in a bad mood than here by herself.

It was an odd realization. Guinevere thought about it some more while she had another scone. She was accustomed to being by herself. She liked her privacy and she liked her own company. It was strange to sit here and realize she'd rather be leafing through a magazine and listening to Zac grumble than shopping on her own.

Damn it, where was this relationship going? More important, what was it doing to her ordered satisfying life? And what on earth had sent her sneaking down the hotel hall last night?

The answers to those questions continued to elude her, and she hadn't had much success in pinning Zac down about them either. Guinevere nursed her tea and continued to gaze out the café window. By now the other executives and their assistants would have checked out of the hotel and would be on the ferry heading home.

Maybe it would be nice to take one more walk down by the marina before she drove Zac's Buick back to the hotel. Guinevere paid her bill, left the tip, and tugged her red trench coat on. Outside on the sidewalk she opened her black umbrella. It wasn't really pouring, just drizzling as she made her way briskly down the street toward the marina. It was nearly empty of people, but the boats were always intriguing, especially when they bobbed on a gray sea against a gray sky. An artist would enjoy the scene, Guinevere reflected. She recalled Vandyke saying once that his wife dabbled in painting.

In the distance she could see Cassidy's Cessna tied up next to the old metal boathouse. She wondered if he ever flew on days like this. Probably. A guy with the right stuff flew in just about any sort of weather. She shook her head at the thought. Being in a small plane was bad enough, flying in one in bad weather seemed sheer stupidity, not to mention terrifying. But she supposed men like Cassidy thrived on terror.

She was gazing at the plane in the distance when she saw a familiar figure climb out of a car in the parking lot and start toward the boathouse. Toby Springer had apparently also been freed for the afternoon by his boss. Idly Guinevere started after him, deciding she'd kill a few more minutes saying hello.

As she watched, he ducked into the boathouse. By the time Guinevere reached the far end of the dock he hadn't reappeared. Maybe Cassidy was also inside the boathouse. Or perhaps Springer was going to take out a boat. She paused, wondering if she should go any farther. If Springer had business with Cassidy, she might just be a nuisance.

Guinevere changed her mind about saying hello. Turning, she started up the ramp. There was an old public toilet on her right. A worn sign on the side nearest her read LADIES in capital letters, and an overflowing trash can guarded the entrance. Guinevere angled around in front of it, following a path that would lead her back toward Zac's car.

As she walked past the far end of the building she glanced back at the boathouse. Cassidy and Springer had both emerged. They were facing each other, and although she couldn't hear what was being said Guinevere got the distinct impression they were arguing.

She also got the impression Cassidy was winning the argument. In fact, she decided as she stood watching them in the shadows of the rest rooms, she would have said Cassidy looked very much like a man giving orders. His hand moved in a flat, negative gesture, and Springer appeared to look resigned. He nodded once, stiff with obvious resentment, and then he swung around and started back toward the parking lot.

Curious, Guinevere switched her gaze back to Cassidy. He was watching Springer, but when the younger man climbed into his car he turned around and walked over to the bobbing Cessna. Opening the craft's door he stood under the high wing and looked around inside the cabin for a moment. Then he shut the door.

As he walked back along the floating dock toward the boathouse Guinevere realized he was carrying a gun. He held it unobtrusively against the right side of his body. No one watching from the marina would have noticed. But from the shadows of the rest rooms Guinevere could see the black metal of the barrel.

She was so startled that she failed to move until Cassidy reappeared from the boathouse. He no longer seemed to be carrying the weapon, unless he'd concealed it somewhere in his clothing. As she watched he ambled leisurely up the ramp and turned left, heading for a small coffee shop that catered to the boating crowd. He had the collar of his flight jacket turned up against the rain but he hadn't bothered with a hat. Dashing—and dangerous.

Guinevere stared at the boathouse and the plane for a very long time. It was getting late, and at this time of year the days were exceedingly short. By four o'clock it was going to be growing dark. There wasn't time to run back to the hotel and convince Zac that he ought to take a look inside that boathouse. If the job was going to get done, Guinevere told herself resolutely, she would have to display a little of the right stuff herself and do it.

She felt the odd little frisson of excitement that she had first known when she'd followed Zac one night during a search he had made of a private house. It was compounded of one part fear, one part adrenaline, and one part thrill. It was heady stuff, but she knew it was also very dangerous. Zac was to blame for having introduced her to it.

Could she make it down to the plane's dock without Cassidy spotting her from the café where he'd gone for coffee? The question was taken out of her hands when Cassidy suddenly emerged from the café and started up the street toward the center of the village.

It was now or never, Guinevere told herself. She emerged cautiously from the protection of the rest rooms and made her way down to the dock. Once on the dock she felt naked and exposed. Anyone who chose to come in this direction from the marina would see her. Halfway along the gently shifting planks Guinevere's heady sense of excitement became two parts fear and one part adrenaline. The thrill was gone.

She couldn't turn back now. She was only a few feet away from the old boathouse. A moment later her hand was on the door. She opened it and quickly stepped through into the dark interior. It took a moment for her eyes to adjust to the dim light seeping through the cracks. In another half hour she wouldn't have been able to see at all, and she wouldn't dare turn on a light if there was one.

A small cabin cruiser was tethered inside the boathouse, but that was all Guinevere could see. Disappointment welled up in her, mitigating the fear. She didn't know what she had expected to find, but she sure hadn't found it. The door closed behind her as she walked over to the cruiser. In the shadows it appeared to be a sleek craft, obviously built for speed.

Guinevere listened for a moment, but all she heard was the rain on the tin roof. Would she be able to hear the sound of approaching footsteps on the dock outside? Even if she did it would be too late to do anything about it. She would be trapped. The only way back to shore was along that narrow dock.

As long as she was here, Guinevere thought, she would just take a quick look inside the boat's cabin. It was a pity to waste the adrenaline. Carefully she eased herself into the boat and made her way to the neat cabin. There wasn't much to see. It looked exactly the same as the cabin of any other small boat. There was no gun casually left lying on the seat.

But then, she told herself, Cassidy wouldn't casually leave a gun lying on the seat. He'd put it somewhere safe. Perhaps a small cupboard or shelf that would be conveniently within reach of the boat's pilot. Remembering to use a handkerchief, Guinevere began cautiously opening doors. She didn't see anything that appeared to be dangerous or incriminating, but in the dim light it was difficult to be sure. She was about to give up when she eased open one last drawer built into the pilot's console. A flat black wallet lay folded inside. She pulled it out and flipped it open.

Luke Cassidy
Drug Enforcement Administration

She barely had time to examine the official-looking identification, which included a picture of Cassidy, when her question about being able to hear footsteps on the dock was answered.

Cassidy's slightly uneven stride was unmistakable, even over the sound of the rain on the roof. Guinevere was trapped, and she knew it. She shoved the leather wallet back into the small drawer and scrambled out of the boat.

And then the excitement that had driven her this far metamorphosed instantly into outright panic.

Chapter Six

The only exit from the boathouse was through the door, unless one counted the water as a potential way out. Guinevere froze on the dock, aware of the deceptively gentle slap of the chilly water against the boat and the wood planks beneath her feet. When she looked down all she could see was endless darkness. The thought of going into that was enough to make her dizzy.

The shock from an unplanned immersion into the cold water would be almost unbearable. The thought of trying to explain her presence in the boathouse to Cassidy was just as unthinkable.

Cassidy's footsteps paused just outside the door.

Summoning up what seemed an incredible amount of willpower Guinevere managed to tiptoe around the dock to the far side of the small cruiser. It's bulk now loomed between her and the door. She crouched in the shadows, praying that Cassidy would not enter the boathouse—or if he did, would not do more than glance casually around. Very little light was seeping into the old structure now. The shadows were welcome.

There was no sound at all from outside the door. Guinevere took several deep breaths and tried to crouch down even more. She was on her knees on the other side of the cruiser. The wooden planks, she discovered to her dismay, were wet, and the dampness was already penetrating the fabric of her pants. The water suddenly seemed very close. The sharp tang of it filled her nostrils.

She ought to get to her feet, march to the door, fling it open, and calmly announce her presence, Guinevere decided resolutely. After all, it wasn't as if she were doing anything terribly illegal. A person could wander into the wrong boathouse by mistake, couldn't she?

Possibly, she answered herself, and then she remembered the brief glimpse of Cassidy's identification. When the boathouse belonged to a man who's profession was hunting drug traffickers, one's explanations had better be pretty damn good. And offhand, she couldn't really think of a damn good explanation.

The image, she reminded herself grimly. She must remember the importance of her tiny but growing, and thus far pristine, business image. It would not be helped by being dragged into a drug smuggling case. Besides, for all she knew Cassidy might not even be willing to listen to explanations. He was obviously working undercover, and the discovery that someone was prowling around his boathouse would be enough to rouse suspicions in even the most even-tempered government man. If only Zac were here. He'd know how to confront Cassidy.

Cassidy's footsteps sounded again. Guinevere heaved a sigh of relief as they moved farther down the dock toward the plane. Hurry up and get what you came for, Cassidy, she thought. I'm getting cold.

There was a large ripple of movement beneath the dock, and water came splashing coldly up between the planks. Was the tide coming in, or was that just a small wave? Guinevere huddled into herself, her hands and feet wet now, as well as the front of her slacks from knee to ankle. She shivered again, and this time it was from something other than fear. The cold water was like ice against her skin.

Stiffly Guinevere changed position slightly, trying to pull the hem of her trench coat around under her knees. It didn't do much good. More water splashed up between the planks. By now, she knew, the sun must have almost disappeared. It was very dark inside the boathouse. A marina light was switched on outside.

There were more sounds along the dock. Cassidy had apparently finished his business with his plane. Leave, Cassidy. Go have a cup of coffee or a beer. Aren't you hungry? Almost dinnertime. His slightly uneven footsteps paused again outside the boathouse door. Guinevere almost tried to make herself invisible by closing her eyes, but forced herself to realize that wasn't going to do the trick. Taking a deep breath she stretched out flat along the planks, praying that the bulk of the boat was high enough to keep him from glancing over onto the other side if he opened the door. She rested her cheek on the dock, and promptly got a splash of icy water in her face. The shock almost made her cry out, and at that moment the door opened. Instinct took over. Guinevere went as still as a newborn fawn hiding from a predator.

A dim unshielded bulb blinked into life overhead. Cassidy came into the boathouse. Guinevere closed her eyes and told herself it was too late now to jump up and yell, "Surprise!" Nothing she could say would make her look innocent. Damn it, Zac. This is your line of work. You're the one who's supposed to be here in this mess, not me.

Another shudder went through her, this time such a mixture of anxiety and cold that she couldn't sort out one sensation from the other. Guinevere waited in an agony of suspense, wondering what it would be like in that instant when Cassidy walked around the dock and found her lying there. She had delayed announcing herself long past the point where she could have made a halfway reasonable explanation. It was too late.

Too late.

The light clicked off and the boathouse was plunged into darkness. At first Guinevere wasn't sure what had happened. She heard the door slam shut and cautiously opened her eyes. Another ripple of water beneath the planks drenched the front of her trench coat and slacks. The cold seemed to be sinking into her.

Cassidy's footsteps dissolved into the distance as he walked back toward shore. Guinevere got painfully to her knees and tried to stand, not sure her legs would hold her. From out of nowhere she remembered that hypothermia didn't result only from immersion in cold water. You could lose body heat to a dangerous degree just by getting yourself damp in weather like this. Her fingers were feeling numb.

She found out how useless numb fingers were when she tried to brace herself against the side of the gently rocking cruiser. When she realized she couldn't feel the fiberglass hull beneath her hand Guinevere almost panicked. Frantically she shook her fingers, trying to generate some sensation. Then she began to worry about her damp feet. She should have worn her boots instead of the casual leather shoes she'd chosen.

Grimly she forced herself to calm down. She was all right. She was shivering a little and her fingers were numb, but she was okay. All she had to do was get back to the Buick and turn on the heater. By the time she arrived at the resort she would be toasty warm. She could have a nice hot cup of tea and perhaps a shot of brandy.

That pleasant scenario required that she first get out of the boathouse, however. Uncertainly Guinevere edged her way around the front of the cruiser and over to the door. She paused a moment, listening intently, and then decided she had to act. Cautiously she opened the door and slipped outside into the chill of early evening. The wind was brisk and it startled her when it struck through the dampness of her clothing. She shivered again, more violently. Light rain slashed at her as she ran for the shelter of the overhang of the rest rooms. From there she tried to peer into the shadows of the parking lot. Was Cassidy out there somewhere keeping an eye on his plane?

She couldn't wait any longer to find out. She was too damn cold. Taking a deep breath, Guinevere ran across the parking lot to the street where she had left the Buick. The physical activity didn't seem to warm her any. It only made her feel more miserable.

She reached the stolidly waiting Buick without incident and fumbled in her purse for the keys. A few moments later she had the car in gear and the heater going full blast. It seemed to take forever to get warm. Guinevere drove away from the village, following the meandering road that led back to the resort.

It was almost completely dark by the time she left Zac's car in the resort parking lot and made her way around to a back entrance. The thought of going through the lobby in her present condition was too much. She would feel a fool.

The car's heater had helped some, but she was still wearing her damp clothing and as she hurried down the corridor to her room Guinevere realized she was still too cold. She had begun shivering again when she got out of the Buick. Feeling a little frantic, she dug the room key out of her purse and twisted it awkwardly in the lock. The phone rang just as she went through the door. She picked up the receiver, knowing who it would be before she answered.

"Jesus Christ, lady, where the hell have you been?"

"Zac, it's a long story, and I'm so cold. Let me get into

a hot shower and get warm. I'll meet you in half an hour down in the lobby."

"The hell you will. I'll be right up." He slammed down the receiver without waiting for an answer.

Sighing, Guinevere went into the bathroom, stripping off her wet clothing. She had the shower on and was just stepping under the blessed warmth when the bathroom door swung open. Guinevere glanced around the curtain to make sure it was Zac. One glance was enough. He was furious.

"How did you get back into the hotel without me seeing you? I've been pacing that damn lobby for forty-five minutes!"

"Please don't yell at me, Zac. I've had a hard afternoon."

"Shopping? Until after dark. When you knew I'd be waiting for you?"

"It's not that late, Zac." She turned her face up into the hot water, considering the nature of his anger. He really had no right to be this upset, she decided. "Worried about your car? It's fine, really."

"I was worried about you." He pushed back the curtain and ran his eyes assessingly over her nakedness. "Your hair looks like hell. What have you been doing?"

She kept her back to him. "Zac, you sound like an irate husband."

"So?" he challenged evenly.

"So back off a little. My patience is just about exhausted. And I'm not accustomed to having men yell at me when I come home a little late."

"I'll bet you're not. You're so goddamn used to doing exactly what you please, when you please, that you—"

"Aren't you?" she interrupted quietly.

To her surprise, that stopped him for a moment. She felt him staring at her, but she didn't turn around. She couldn't turn around, actually. The hot water was finally beginning to warm her. Nothing had ever felt so good as this shower.

"Yeah," he finally said. "I guess I am. I guess we're both accustomed to setting our own rules." He drew a long breath. "Okay, Gwen, I won't yell. But that was my car you disappeared in. I think I deserve an explanation, don't you?"

"I hate it when you get reasonable. Takes all the fun out of arguing with you." But she knew her voice lacked any real sting of flippancy. She sounded as weary as she suddenly felt. "Zac, could you order me a cup of tea from room service? I really did get cold. A little too cold, I think."

He must have sensed the seriousness of the situation. With a last assessing glance he dropped the shower curtain, and a moment later she heard the bathroom door close.

Zac was just pouring a cup of hot tea as she emerged from the bathroom swathed in her robe. He swung around and strode across the room, thrusting the warm cup into her hands.

"Here. Drink this."

She sipped gratefully at the tea, feeling its warmth heating her from within. "Stop glowering, Zac. I'm okay. And I'm sorry you were worried. Am I really that late?"

"Considering the fact that I was expecting you sometime between three and three thirty, yes. I was about to borrow Vandyke's Mercedes and come looking for you. What the hell happened? How did you get so cold?"

Wearily Guinevere sank down onto the edge of the bed, her teacup cradled in her hands. "It's going to sound silly when I tell you. Promise me you won't start yelling?"

He sat in the chair across from the bed, gray eyes pinning her. "I never make promises I can't be sure of keeping. Talk. Was it an accident with the car?"

"Your precious Buick is fine. The truth is, I got trapped in Cassidy's boathouse."

There was a split second of silence that seemed as heavy as lead. The gray gaze was unwavering. "With Cassidy?"

Realizing his conclusion, Guinevere hastily shook her head. "No. Zac, you're not going to like the way I did it but I think I've got some answers. I took a little walk down to the marina shortly after three. Guess who I saw talking to Cassidy?"

"Who?"

"Toby Springer. But this time it didn't look as if they were arranging an outing. They seemed to be arguing."

"Where were you that you could see that much?"

"Standing in the shadow of the public rest rooms. Exciting, huh? I had no idea this investigative business was so glamorous. At any rate they both left, and—"

"Together?"

She shook her head. "Toby left first and then Cassidy. I assumed they were gone for the evening so I decided to have a quick look around that boathouse."

Zac closed his eyes, apparently pleading silently for patience. "I should have guessed."

"It's your fault. You're the one who taught me these devious little tricks."

"I've created a monster," he groaned. Then, curiosity getting the better of him, he asked reluctantly, "Well? Find anything?"

"A boat."

"Not an unlikely object to find in a boathouse."

Guinevere paused for effect. "There was a leather wallet in the boat, Zac."

"Oh, hell. You went through the boat?"

"It seemed like the logical thing to do. I said to myself, what would Zac do if he were here? You were my inspiration."

"Okay, I can see you're dying to spring the surprise. What was in the wallet?"

"I.D. for one Luke Cassidy. He's government, Zac. Drug Enforcement Administration."

"Shit."

"I felt a little nervous myself. I was about to make a strategic retreat when I heard him returning along the dock. I made it to the other side of the boat and crouched down behind it. That's how I got so cold and damp. The water kept splashing up between the planks. And when he came into the boathouse and turned on the light—"

"He found you?" Zac's gaze was riveted to her face.

"No. I nearly panicked. It was a horrible sensation, Zac. Only the thought of the image kept me from jumping up and throwing myself on the mercy of the government. Can you imagine? How would I have ever explained my snooping around in the boathouse of a government agent? Camelot Services would have undoubtedly come under all sorts of suspicion. It would have been embarrassing and humiliating and I might have ended up in jail or something. I can just see the headlines: Owner of Small Temporary-Employment Firm Linked to Drug Case."

"So you stayed put and managed to get yourself chilled to the bone instead? You were willing to risk hypothermia for the image?"

"I know it sounds dumb now, but at the time . . ." She morosely let the sentence trail off and took another sip of tea. She was finally beginning to feel comfortably warm again.

Zac got to his feet, shoving his hands into his hip pockets. Restlessly he stalked to the window. "You may have been right. Staying out of sight may have been the best option under the circumstances. But, Jesus, Gwen!"

"I know."

He turned to face her, his expression hard. "So he's DEA?"

"That's what the identification said. Had a little picture of him and everything."

"Damn."

"You're doing a lot of swearing tonight."

"Yeah. I'm feeling put-upon." He glanced back at the darkness beyond the window. "We're in the middle of something, Gwen, and I don't like it. Best option for us right now is to get the hell out of here."

She studied him worriedly. "Middle of what?"

He sighed, swinging around once more to confront her. "I heard from Sol late this afternoon."

"Your friend Sol in Saint Thomas?"

Zac nodded brusquely. "He said a man named Gannon and one named Edward Vandyke were partners a few years back in a small charter operation that was based on Saint Thomas. The business was closed shortly after Gannon was killed."

"All right. That fits with what Vandyke told us." Guinevere eyed Zac curiously. "So what's the catch?"

"According to the information Sol dug up, there was a suspicion that the Gannon-Vandyke charter service made money flying more than passengers and cargo."

Guinevere bit her lip, guessing what was coming next. "Drugs?"

Zac paced back to the chair and sat down slowly. "The authorities never uncovered any proof, and no charges were ever brought. Sol said it was just speculation. A lot of people with airplanes come under suspicion down in the Caribbean. There are a lot of pilots in that part of the world involved in the South American drug chain. The runs are extremely lucrative. A couple of big ones and a man would have a nice bit of capital. He might have enough cash to invest in a legitimate business, for instance. A business such as Vandyke Development."

"Or he might get killed," Guinevere said slowly. "The way Gannon did?"

Zac looked at her for a moment. "Actually, the way Gannon got killed raises some interesting questions."

"Didn't Vandyke tell the truth?"

"Sol says that according to the reports in the local paper, which he found in the library, Gannon went down in April of nineteen seventy-two. Apparently he dumped the plane in the water off some little island called Raton. It's an uninhabited place, a chunk of rock in the Caribbean. The authorities eventually found traces of the wreckage. The body was never recovered."

Guinevere frowned. "Okay, it all still fits."

Zac watched her through narrowed eyes. "Not quite. Remember the photocopied page of Gannon's logbook? The one we found in Vandyke's briefcase?"

She nodded. "I remember. What about it?"

"It shows another flight, in May of that year. One month after Gannon is supposed to have disappeared."

"Oh my God, that's right. I'd forgotten." Guinevere sat stunned, absorbing the implications. "And that last entry was filled out in the same handwriting as the previous entries, wasn't it? At least, I don't remember thinking at the time that it appeared to be different handwriting."

Zac inclined his head once, leaning back in the chair with his big hands linked together under his chin. The gray gaze was almost remote now. Guinevere had seen that look before, and it made her uneasy.

"So," he went on almost musingly, "we have one very nervous ex-partner of a man who may not be dead. And the partnership may have been involved in drug smuggling. We also have a dashing pilot running around who apparently is familiar with Toby Springer and Washburn. Said pilot is carrying DEA identification."

Guinevere shivered again, but not from cold. "I think you're right, Zac. I think we are in the middle of something. Something messy." She paused a moment, her mind skipping ahead. "Do you think it's the fact that Gannon might be alive that's upsetting our client?"

"He's running scared from something. If he'd been under the impression that his ex-partner was dead all these years, and then someone sends him a page out of a logbook with a flight filled in *after* the one that should have been the last . . ."

"You think Gannon's materialized from Vandyke's past and is going to blackmail Vandyke?"

Zac shrugged. "It's one possibility, and it would explain a lot. Vandyke's straight these days. He's built up a good business. He's about to conclude a very important deal."

"Rumors of a past spent smuggling drugs could ruin him in the Seattle business community," Guinevere concluded thoughtfully.

"Talk about having your image tarnished."

"Yes."

They sat in silence for a while, considering the situation. Finally Zac spoke. "I don't think it's the documents he's worried about. I think he's been trying to get bodyguard service without telling me that's what he really needs. He only seems to be concerned about the briefcase when I remind him of it. The rest of the time he's distracted and nervous, and he doesn't like me to get too far out of sight."

"A bodyguard? To protect him from a blackmailer?"

"A possibility."

"And in the meantime the Drug Enforcement Administration is breathing down his neck?"

Zac winced. "Poor Vandyke. He's got more reason to be nervous than he even knows. You said Toby Springer was arguing with Cassidy?"

Guinevere nodded thoughtfully. "It's not the first time I've seen them together. Remember when we first saw him standing on Cassidy's dock?"

"Yeah." Zac idly rubbed his thumb along his jaw, eyes distant. "If Toby Springer is working with Cassidy then we have to assume someone is setting a trap."

"But for whom? Vandyke's been legitimate for years. Would they really waste a lot of time and money coming down on him now?"

"The government never needs an excuse to waste tax dollars, you know that," Zac replied impatiently. "But you're right. It would seem more likely they'd be interested in a current case, not one that was over a decade old."

"I can't believe Vandyke is currently involved in smuggling dope!" Guinevere was incensed at the notion. "He's a nice man, Zac. He's got a wife he cares about, a good reputation, a successful business—"

"That business may have been founded on the proceeds of his last smuggling venture," Zac reminded her bluntly. "He may have decided to go back to his old line of work for new capital."

"I refuse to believe it!"

"That's because you don't want to believe it. You like the guy."

"What's wrong with liking him?" she fumed.

"In your case, it tends to cloud your reasoning. You're too empathic, Gwen. You let your emotions dictate your loyalties."

She stared at him, infuriated. "What a chauvinistic

thing to say! Just because I tend to trust my judgments of people, that doesn't mean I let my emotions sway those judgments! I like Edward Vandyke, and I don't believe he's involved in drug smuggling—whatever he may or may not have done in the past."

"Your faith in your client is touching. But it doesn't solve our immediate problem."

"What is our immediate problem? Warning Vandyke about Cassidy?"

Zac gave her a dryly amused look. "If you think Vandyke is an innocent honest businessman, why are you concerned with warning him about Cassidy? Why would he even need to be warned about him?"

Guinevere flushed, aware of the trap he was setting. "He's a client of mine. I feel obliged to help him. And you should feel the same, Zac. Vandyke's your client too."

"One who hasn't been straightforward with me."

"He's scared!"

"That's not my problem, unless he chooses to be up-front about the situation and unless he hires me to do something about it. Even at that point I'm not obliged to worry about it unless I decide to take the case. Gwen, as far as I'm concerned, Vandyke hired me to baby-sit a briefcase full of documents. So far nothing has happened to that briefcase. I've done my job. And you've done everything you were obligated to do. I have a feeling it's time for both of us to get the hell out of Dodge City."

"What do you mean?"

"I mean you and I should be on the next ferry back to Anacortes." He glanced at his black metal wristwatch. "It leaves in an hour. If we move, we can make it."

Guinevere set down her teacup, alarmed. "Zac, we can't just leave like that. We've got to talk to Vandyke."

"Honey, we don't have the least idea of what's coming

down here. Cassidy might be planning some kind of raid. He might be setting a trap. And who the hell knows where Toby Springer fits into all this?"

A thought struck Guinevere. "What if Springer is a plant?" she asked, her eyes wide. "Maybe he's working for Cassidy's outfit as an inside informant."

Zac looked exasperated. "Wonderful. And where does that lead us? Do we then assume that Sheldon Washburn is cooperating with the government? Helping Cassidy set up Vandyke?"

Guinevere bit her lip. "Not necessarily. Washburn and Vandyke are going to be partners after the final contracts are signed," she went on slowly. "Maybe they've been partners before."

Zac considered that. "You think Washburn might be Gannon?"

"Why not? It's a possibility, isn't it? Washburn and Vandyke are in similar lines of work these days—real estate development. They've both emerged on the business scene since nineteen seventy-two, and they both seem to have had a good chunk of capital with which to get started. It would be easy enough for them to pretend in front of the rest of us that they've never met before."

"Oh great, Gwen. Now you're not only convicting your own client, you're saying Washburn's in on it with him. Make up your mind."

She stood up. "I can't make up my mind. I don't know what's going on. And neither do you. We can't just leave Vandyke in this situation, Zac. We've got to at least talk to him."

"No we don't."

Guinevere glared at him over her shoulder as she crossed the small room to her closet and began searching for something to wear to dinner. "He's our client, Zac."

"We're not doctors, priests, or lawyers. Our relationship with a client is hardly sacred."

"Do you mean to sit there and tell me we're going to do absolutely nothing for Vandyke? Just hop on the next ferry and get ourselves safely out of the picture."

"It would seem," he said, "the most advisable course of action at the moment. I don't have any desire to be blithely sitting in the middle of this mess sipping tea when Cassidy comes through the front door, six-guns blazing. As you discovered in the boathouse, the prospect of explaining our innocence to the government is about as enthralling as explaining our tax returns to them at an audit."

Guinevere studied his face, seeing the resolve in his eyes. "Vandyke's a client, Zac," she said quietly, reaching into the closet to pull out a black wool dress. "I think we owe him the courtesy of offering him your services."

Zac looked as if he hadn't heard her correctly. "What's this? We owe him the courtesy of offering him *my* services? In what capacity, for God's sake? I'm a consultant, not a hired gun. And above all I will not allow you to get further involved in this damn situation."

"Zac, all I'm asking is that we talk to him. Tonight. We can leave in the morning after we've fulfilled our obligations."

Zac threw up his hands and surged out of the chair. "You're a stubborn, idiotic, emotional, bleeding-heart female who doesn't have the common sense she was born with. What's worse, you're trying to drag me down with you. If *I* had the sense I was born with I'd bundle you up, stuff you into the car, drive you onto that ferry, and say the hell with it."

Guinevere looked at him hopefully. "We'll talk to Vandyke?"

"*I'll* talk to Vandyke. You will keep your charming

little ass out of this, or I will not be responsible for what happens. When it comes to security matters that turkey is my client, not yours. Got it?"

"Thank you, Zac." Guinevere demurely lowered her eyes so that he wouldn't see her satisfaction. She scurried into the bathroom to dress for dinner.

Chapter Seven

There were times, Zac reflected a few hours later, when he'd give anything to have Gwen's winning way with people, when he would find it very useful to have them confide as easily in him as they often did in her. Theoretically he should have had Gwen with him when he tried to pin down his anxiety-ridden client. She always had a soothing effect on people. But the truth was he didn't dare get her any more involved in this crazy situation than she already was. Furthermore, if Vandyke was enmeshed in some drug-running scam the last thing Zac wanted was for his client to think he and Gwen were aware of it. People who ran drugs were inclined to be defensive on occasion. Downright hostile, in fact. The simple truth was, people who ran drugs were often willing to kill to protect their lucrative secrets. No, Zac decided, if Vandyke was innocent, and genuinely needed help, the man was going to have to volunteer more information.

By ten thirty that evening Zac had to admit that thus far the gentle art of subtle interrogation was not going well. He was fairly good at the straightforward pin-them-to-the-wall style, but he lacked the finesse needed for the more diplomatic strategy. He ordered another tequila and watched Guinevere dancing with Toby Springer. The sight annoyed him, but he had to admit it kept her occupied and away from the table while he was trying to corner Vandyke. Beside him Vandyke watched the pair on the dance floor broodingly. Washburn had retired a half hour earlier. Zac decided to make one more attempt with Vandyke.

"With your competitors gone, and now that you and Washburn have signed the development deal, I can't see any further need to worry about that briefcase, Mr. Vandyke. I think I'll let you keep it tonight."

"Fine." Vandyke sounded uninterested. He was still watching Guinevere and Springer.

"I thought Gwen and I could catch the first ferry out in the morning."

That caught Vandyke's attention. "You're going back early? I thought we agreed you'd stay until I'm ready to return to Seattle. I was planning on leaving around noon. Actually, I had planned to discuss the possibility of your continuing to—"

"I've got a business to run, and it really doesn't look as if you need me any longer," Zac said ruthlessly. He looked at the older man. "I'm not sure you ever needed me in the first place. No one so much as winked at that damn briefcase."

Vandyke shifted his glance back to the dance floor. "Having you along was just a precaution."

"Against what?"

"You know. Theft, industrial espionage, that sort of thing. You can't be too careful these days."

Zac held on to his patience. "Why don't we level with each other, Vandyke. If you're in trouble, tell me. You're my client. I'll do my best to help you. But don't give me any more bull about that damn briefcase. You were never all that concerned about it. You just wanted me nearby. Somehow I can't believe you were simply looking for companionship."

Vandyke stiffened. "Nobody's paying you to ask questions, Justis."

"I know. I'm being paid to stick close. Not to the briefcase, but to you. Why don't you be honest about that part, at least? Normally I don't hire myself out as a bodyguard. It lacks class."

"Now listen here, Justis—"

"But since I'm already on the scene, I'll do what I can —if you'll tell me what it is I'm supposed to be guarding you against," Zac concluded coldly.

"I don't have the vaguest idea what you're talking about."

Zac wanted to slam the man up against a wall. His fingers tightened around the small tequila glass. "If it's blackmail, Vandyke, there are ways of dealing with it."

Vandyke's eyes widened for an instant and then narrowed. His voice was tight. "You're way out of line even suggesting that I'm being blackmailed. What the hell gave you that idea? I have absolutely nothing to hide. I resent your implication, Justis."

Zac cradled his tequila in both hands, his elbows on the table, studying the older man for a long moment. This was getting nowhere. "All right, Vandyke. Have it your way. You hired a baby-sitter for that briefcase for three days. You've had your money's worth. I'm leaving first thing in the morning and I'm taking Gwen with me."

"I was under the impression Miss Jones was an independent businesswoman," Vandyke snapped. "She doesn't work for you."

"No, but in this situation she'll do what I tell her."

"Why should she do that, Justis?"

"Because if she doesn't I'll pick her up and carry her on board that ferry tomorrow morning. I'm not leaving

112

her here with you when I can't figure out what the hell is going down."

"Does Miss Jones know your intentions?" Vandyke murmured sarcastically as Guinevere and Toby Springer approached the table.

Guinevere smiled, her eyes bright with charming inquiry. "Does Miss Jones know what intentions?" Springer pulled out a chair for her before Zac could get to his feet. Then the younger man sat down beside her. Zac felt his irritation rise.

"I was just telling Mr. Vandyke that you and I will be leaving first thing in the morning." He watched Guinevere coolly, silently challenging her to defy the edict.

Guinevere hesitated, and Zac saw the concern in her face. She knew he had failed. For a moment he thought she would refuse to cooperate, but she smiled ruefully at her client. "I'm afraid Zac's right. I've already stayed longer than I should. I promised my sister I would be back in the office tomorrow morning, and I won't be able to get there until tomorrow afternoon as it is."

"I'm paying you for your time, Miss Jones," Vandyke said huffily. "I don't see the problem."

"It's a scheduling problem," Guinevere explained quite gently. "My sister is only helping out, you see. She isn't a full-time employee of Camelot Services. I really must get back. And Zac has a business to run too. He took this job for you as a favor to me, but he made it clear from the outset he couldn't commit to more than three or four days. Isn't that right, Zac?"

"Right." He was vastly relieved that she didn't intend to fight him on this. "We'll leave in the morning." He glanced at his watch. "That first ferry is a very early one. We'd better head for bed." He got pointedly to his feet and waited for Guinevere. Toby Springer looked dismayed.

113

"Hey," Springer protested, jumping up to pull out Guinevere's chair. "How about one last dance?"

Zac already had his hand under Guinevere's arm. "I think Gwen's as ready for bed as I am, aren't you, Gwen," he answered for her.

"Well, actually, it is only ten thirty, and I"—she gave a small cough as Zac tightened his hold on her arm—"I did have a busy afternoon. I think I will retire. Good night, Mr. Vandyke. I probably won't see you in the morning. Have a good trip back to Seattle, and congratulations on concluding the deal with Washburn." She nodded politely at Toby Springer and allowed herself to be hauled forcibly out of the lounge.

"Really, Zac," she muttered as he marched her down the corridor to her room, "there's no need to be so heavy-handed about this."

"Probably not. But it comes naturally to me."

She shot him a swift glance as he took the key from her hand and turned it in the lock. There was a new remoteness in his eyes. It was the expression she'd seen during the last stages of the StarrTech case. She'd mentally labeled it Justis in Deep Think. He was just going into it now, and if she didn't catch him quickly he would be too far-gone to deal with.

"No luck with Vandyke?" she demanded as she preceded Zac into the room.

"No."

The monosyllabic answer was not a good sign. Zac was more far-gone than she had thought. "Did you confront him with what we knew?"

Zac stood by the door, staring thoughtfully at the blank television screen across the room. "We don't know much."

"I realize that, but did you imply we knew he might be in real trouble?"

"I asked him if he was being blackmailed."

Guinevere perked up. "What did he say?"

"Denied it."

"Did you tell him about Cassidy?"

"No."

Impatiently Guinevere tossed her purse onto the dresser. "Well, why not?"

"If Vandyke's running drugs, I don't want him knowing we know. Not unless he's willing to confide in us first."

Hands on hips, Guinevere faced him, but first she had to get between him and the television set. "I see. A standoff, is that it? You wouldn't tell him how much we knew, so he decided to play it cool too. The result is that neither of you got anywhere because you wouldn't take the risk of confiding in each other. I knew I shouldn't have left the confrontation to you, Zac. I should have handled it myself."

Zac's eyes focused long enough to meet her irate gaze. "Don't be stupid, Gwen. There's more at stake here than trying to help a client who doesn't want too much help. We're better off out of this, and you know it."

Guinevere lapsed into silence herself after that. Zac was probably right, she realized morosely as she drifted around the room packing her suitcase, lost in a sensation of uneasy regret. Still, it just didn't seem proper to be abandoning Vandyke to his fate this way.

It was when she was getting ready to brush her teeth that Guinevere finally became aware that Zac was showing no signs of going back to his own room. He was still sprawled in the chair he had sunk into shortly after arriving, and his attention was still focused on something she couldn't see.

"Zac?"

No response.

Guinevere crossed the room to stand in front of him. "Zac? Aren't you going to go to bed?"

He blinked and looked up at her briefly. "No. I'm just going to sit here and think for a while."

"All night?"

He shrugged and went back to thinking.

Guinevere sighed and headed for the bathroom. When she emerged in her nightgown a few minutes later he hadn't moved. Tentatively Guinevere switched off the light. There was no word of protest from Zac. Deep Think had taken over completely. Either that or he was asleep. Guinevere gave up and crawled into bed.

She didn't look at the clock when the bed gave beneath Zac's weight a long time later. Guinevere stirred, feeling the pleasant heat of his body as he curled against her, and went back to sleep. Her last fleeting thought was that there was a deep sense of comfort to be found going to sleep in Zac's arms.

It was still dark when the ferry left shortly after six the next morning. Zac must have set an alarm, Guinevere decided, although she hadn't heard it. Of course, at that hour she would have been lucky to hear the Seattle Symphony if it had been playing right there in the hotel room. She was still yawning as she followed Zac up from the ferry's car deck and stumbled into the cafeteria.

"Sit here and I'll get us some coffee. Do you want anything to eat? We've got nearly a two-hour trip ahead of us." He frowned down at her as she slipped into a booth.

Guinevere shook her head. "Just bring on the caffeine."

He nodded and left, returning a few minutes later with two plastic cups. "Here you go," he said, and set one down in front of her.

116

"You weren't kidding when you said this ferry left early. It's still the middle of the night outside." She sipped the coffee gratefully. "Ah, that's better. Come to any momentous conclusions last night?"

Zac looked at her. "Not really. Just a lot of questions. Nothing new about those. I've had them all along."

"It still doesn't feel right."

"Ditching Vandyke?" Zac grimaced. "I know. I hate to admit it, but it does feel wrong somehow. I sort of liked the guy. But that's the thing about criminals, Gwen. They're incredible con men. If they weren't, they wouldn't get away with everything, up to and including murder."

"Vandyke is no murderer!"

"I was just making a generalization, honey. Calm down."

Silence prevailed for another few minutes as they drank their coffee. Then Zac said carefully, "I did some thinking about that wild hypothesis you had. The one about Washburn possibly being Vandyke's old partner, Gannon."

Guinevere felt a flicker of interest. "Did you?"

"With all those papers you were handling for Vandyke you didn't by any chance happen to end up with anything that might have Washburn's handwriting on it, did you? Notes he might have made, or his signature?"

Guinevere's eyes widened in admiration. "Zac, that's a brilliant idea. We could compare his handwriting to the handwriting on that page from Gannon's logbook." Her face fell. "If we still had the page from the logbook."

There was a significant pause from the other side of the table. "We've got it."

"We do? Zac, you copied it?"

He shrugged one shoulder a bit too casually. "I had a lot of time on my hands at certain points during the weekend, and the hotel had a self-service photocopy machine. Yesterday while you were playing hide-and-seek with Cassidy I got bored enough to use the machine."

"Let's see the page." Eagerly Guinevere leaned forward.

"First we'll need a sample of Washburn's handwriting."

"Oh, right. Got it here, I think." Guinevere rummaged around in her oversize shoulder bag for some stray envelopes and documents she had collected during the stay at the resort. "I have his signature on some of the drafts of the final letter of agreement he drew up with Vandyke. Here!" Triumphantly she pulled an envelope out of her purse.

Zac reached for the letter, opening it with slick efficiency. "Have you ever emptied that purse since the day you bought it?" he asked.

"I never empty a purse completely until I buy a new one. Let's see that page from the logbook."

He pulled a folded sheet of paper from his jacket pocket and spread it out on the table. "You realize this isn't exactly foolproof? I'm no handwriting expert. We won't be absolutely sure, even if the writing does seem similar."

"Stop being a pessimist. Let's have a look."

But one glance was all Guinevere needed. She looked at the flamboyant scrawl in which the logbook had been filled out, and then at Washburn's neat precise signature. "Well, so much for that brilliant theory. There's no similarity at all. No one's handwriting could change that much in the course of a decade." She frowned. "Or could it?"

Zac didn't look up from studying the two samples. "It's possible, if he made a deliberate attempt to alter his handwriting. But I don't think that's the case here. It would take an expert to be sure, though. On the face of it, I'd have to conclude Washburn is not Gannon."

"Ah, well. It was an interesting idea. What could we have done even if we'd decided he was Gannon?"

Zac's mouth crooked. "Not much. It would have been one more reason for staying out of Hopalong Cassidy's way."

"Because it would have meant Vandyke and Gannon had decided to go back into business together?"

"Mmm. And that Cassidy has probably set them both up for a fall."

"Now what do we conclude? That Cassidy has probably set up just our client?" Guinevere downed the rest of her coffee, aware of a deep feeling of anger. "I think we should have warned Vandyke."

Zac did a short staccato drumroll with his fingers on the table. "If the guy's running drugs, Gwen . . ."

"I know. But I don't think he is. He just isn't the type."

"Gwen—"

"I *know* he isn't. His wife is too nice and he's too worried about saving their relationship. A drug runner wouldn't give a damn about that sort of thing, would he? He'd just replace the wife with a cute teenybopper or something."

Zac's brows shot upward. "No kidding?"

"I'm serious, Zac."

He sighed. "So am I."

"So what do we do?" she asked challengingly.

Zac did the drumroll with his left hand. "That's what I've been asking myself all night."

Guinevere felt a spark of hope. "Let's go back and talk to him, Zac."

"We're halfway to Anacortes. It will take us another

hour to get there and then nearly two hours to get back on the next ferry."

"We'll call him from Anacortes."

"Gwen, I'm not sure he wants our help. That's what's worrying me. I get the distinct impression the guy wants us to back off."

"We have to tell him about Cassidy," Guinevere said with grave resolution. "We owe our client that much, Zac."

Zac groaned and surrendered. "Okay. I'll call him when we reach Anacortes."

But an hour later when they drove off the ferry in Anacortes and found a telephone the Good Samaritan project went down the tubes.

"There's no answer, and the front desk says they tried a page." Zac stepped out of the phone booth.

"Then we'll have to get right back on that ferry," Guinevere announced, feeling committed now.

"It would make more sense to try phoning every half hour," Zac pointed out.

"I think we should go back." She faced him determinedly. "I want to talk to him in person."

"I know I'm going to regret this," Zac murmured.

The return trip seemed to take forever, but three and a half hours after they had left the island Zac was driving the Buick back off the ferry. He took the first turn to the left and started toward the resort. He had said very little during the return trip, but he did glance casually at the marina as they drove past the dock where Cassidy kept his plane.

"The Cessna's gone."

Guinevere peered out the window. "What do you suppose that means?"

Zac abruptly increased the speed of the Buick, saying nothing.

By the time he finally parked in front of the resort Guinevere was more than uneasy, she was downright nervous. Zac quietly reached out and took her hand as they walked into the lobby.

"Hey, settle down. It's going to be okay. We'll deliver our grand message and then leave. We'll have done our duty by our client."

"I'm worried, Zac."

"So am I," he admitted. He released her hand and headed for the front desk. The clerk looked up in surprise.

"Oh, Mr. Justis. I thought you'd checked out this morning."

"I did. I'm back. I'm trying to locate Mr. Vandyke. Have you seen him this morning?"

The clerk nodded. "A couple of hours ago. He checked out too."

"Did he?" Zac leaned forward, his hands on the polished countertop. "Did he sign the bill?"

"Well, not exactly. Mr. Springer checked out for both Mr. Washburn and Mr. Vandyke."

"They left a couple hours ago? That wouldn't mesh with any of the ferry schedules."

The clerk was looking increasingly confused. "I believe Mr. Springer said that Washburn and Vandyke were in a hurry to get back to the mainland. They were going to hire a charter flight."

"Really? And what did Vandyke intend to do with his car?"

Confusion turned to nervousness mingled with belligerence on the clerk's face. Zac's relentless, undiplomatic approach was beginning to have its usual effect, and Guinevere decided she'd better step in. Smiling brilliantly she went to the counter.

"Don't pay any attention to him," she advised the

clerk. He blinked warily. "He gets a little overbearing at times. We're trying to find Mr. Vandyke because something very crucial has arisen. A business matter. It's imperative that we find him. You say he and Washburn intended to fly out this morning?"

"That's what Mr. Springer said." The clerk kept an eye on Zac, who was still glaring at him.

"Then I guess we've missed him." Guinevere turned away from the desk. "Thanks for your help," she added over her shoulder, making a grab for Zac's arm and leading him out of earshot. "So much for that. There's no sense hounding him, Zac. He doesn't know anything."

"Vandyke told us he doesn't fly in small planes anymore," Zac said, looking down at her.

"I remember," Guinevere whispered.

"But the clerk thinks he hired a plane with Washburn this morning," Zac continued flatly.

"And Cassidy's plane is gone." Guinevere twisted her hands together as she wandered over to stand in front of the lobby fireplace. Zac followed slowly. A few other guests were lounging in chairs, reading and sipping coffee. It was a warm and peaceful winter scene, but Guinevere did not feel at all peaceful. "If Cassidy has moved in on our client already," she murmured, "would he have flown Vandyke someplace after arresting him? Wouldn't he have called in the local authorities?"

"Who the hell knows. Cassidy seems like the independent type. Not an overly cooperative sort. He'd want the excitement and glory of the kill." Zac rested a hand on Guinevere's shoulder as he stood staring down into the fire. "But he'd probably dump Vandyke into the laps of the local cops. The lion bringing in his prey so that everyone could admire him. He'd just want to be certain he got all the credit."

Guinevere slanted a curious glance at Zac. "You don't think much of Cassidy, do you?"

"He's a hot dog." Zac moved abruptly, taking Guinevere by surprise. "Come on."

"Where are we going?"

"To the marina. I want to have a look in that boathouse. If Cassidy's got his plane in the air this should be a good time to have another look around."

"But, Zac—" Guinevere began, but stopped as she noticed the clerk at the front desk signaling her. He had a phone in one hand and he was beckoning her with the other. "Miss Jones?"

Hastily Guinevere went forward. "What is it? Is that Vandyke on the line?"

Holding his palm over the receiver, the clerk shook his head. He looked anxious. "Mrs. Vandyke. She insists on speaking to her husband. I've told her he's gone, but she says—"

"I'll talk to her." Guinevere took the phone. "Mrs. Vandyke? This is Guinevere Jones, the temporary secretary your husband hired this past week. I spoke to you briefly on the phone on a couple of occasions."

"Yes, Miss Jones, I remember. Where is my husband?" The woman's voice was laced with concern. She sounded tired and more than a little scared.

"I'm trying to locate him myself. The front desk says he hired a plane this morning to take him back to Seattle."

Catherine Vandyke jumped on that announcement. "A plane? What sort of plane?"

Guinevere took a breath, her eyes meeting Zac's intent gaze. "A small plane, we think. Perhaps a Cessna One Eighty-five."

"That's impossible. My husband would never set foot

123

in such a small plane. He hates them. Used to fly them, you know."

"I believe he did say something about it once."

"Well, he doesn't fly in them anymore. He must be around there someplace, Miss Jones. Please find him. Besides, he couldn't want to fly back to Seattle. What would he do with the Mercedes? He told me he was taking the ferry to the San Juans."

"Yes, Mrs. Vandyke, he did. Listen, I wonder if you could tell me——" Guinevere broke off in surprise as the phone was deftly removed from her hand.

Zac held the receiver to his ear, one hand braced against the desk. "Mrs. Vandyke, this is Zachariah Justis. I've been employed by your husband for the past few days. He hired me to do some security consultation. . . . Yes, that's right. . . . No, I don't know why he would need someone like me. I do have a few hunches. I thought maybe you could tell me. . . . Are you absolutely certain your husband wouldn't willingly fly in a small plane?" There was another pause while he got the short, apparently affirmative response. Zac drew a breath. "Okay, I've got a couple of questions. They're going to seem a little off the wall, but if you'll answer them I might have a shot at locating Vandyke."

Guinevere stirred restlessly, frowning. She should probably be dealing with the woman, she decided. Zac could be so heavy-handed at times.

"Were you married to your husband when he had that charter operation down in the Caribbean, Mrs. Vandyke? . . . I see. Do you remember his partner, a man named Gannon?" Zac listened for a moment and then held the phone away from his ear. Helplessly he held it out to Guinevere. "She's gone hysterical on me."

Guinevere took the phone. On the other end Catherine Vandyke was in pieces. There were tears and fury in her voice. "What are you talking about? How do you know about Gannon? This is ridiculous. I insist you put my husband on the phone, or I'll call the police. Do you hear me?"

"Mrs. Vandyke, this is Guinevere again. Please listen to me. Zac is only trying to help. We know your husband is in trouble, but we don't know what kind."

"But he can't be in trouble," the other woman wailed. "Gannon's dead. He's been dead all these years."

"We have reason to think he might be alive. If he were alive, Mrs. Vandyke, would he be a threat to your husband?" Guinevere looked at Zac to see if she was asking the right questions. Zac was furiously scribbling a note on a pad of hotel paper.

"Oh, God, I don't even want to think about it." Mrs. Vandyke sounded terrified now.

"Listen to me, Mrs. Vandyke. You've got to think about it. You've got to help us, or your husband might wind up in real trouble. Zac can help him. It's his business. But he needs some answers. Please tell me about Gannon."

There was a sob on the other end of the line, and then Mrs. Vandyke caught her breath. Guinevere could almost see her pulling herself together, rallying to meet the crisis.

"Gannon was my husband's partner."

"We know that much."

"He . . . he used to claim he loved me."

Guinevere said nothing, listening to her strengthening voice.

"That was a long time ago," Mrs. Vandyke whispered. "We were all much younger then. More reckless. More adventurous. But Gannon was more than that. He was— well, wild in some ways. Always living an adventure. Bigger than life. He thrived on danger and excitement. And he thought he was irresistible where women were concerned."

"I understand," Guinevere said softly.

"He never could see why I preferred Edward. Edward was the businessman of the two. The one who kept the records, got the contracts, met the schedules. Gannon took the chances. Edward was quieter. And I knew Edward loved me. A woman could never be first in Gannon's life. Do you know what I mean, Miss Jones? Gannon would always put himself and his need for adventure first. And he could be vicious."

Guinevere felt herself grow suddenly cold. "Vicious?"

"I'll tell you something I've never told anyone else, Miss Jones. The truth is, the day I learned Gannon had gone down I felt an indescribable relief. He had been so angry the day he left. Edward and I had just decided to get married, and we made the announcement the night before Gannon's last flight. I'll never forget the way Gannon stormed out of the little restaurant where we'd all gone for dinner. Early the next morning before he left he found me. I worked in a little boutique there on Saint Thomas. He walked into the shop, dragged me out from behind the counter, and told me that when he got back things were going to be different. He swore I was going to marry him, not Edward, and he'd make sure of it, regardless of who got in the way. I was scared, Miss Jones. There was something in his eyes that morning. I knew he wasn't really so madly in love with me that he couldn't bear to think of me marrying another man. It was his damn pride that was hurt. Gannon was so . . . so supremely . . . what do they call it these days?"

"Macho." Guinevere shuddered. The picture forming in her mind was not at all reassuring. She knew another man who fit Mrs. Vandyke's image of the mysterious Gannon.

"Yes, macho. He frightened me that morning, Miss Jones. I began to worry about what he might do to Edward when he returned. But he never returned."

"Mrs. Vandyke, how old would Gannon be now?" Guinevere read the question off of the notepad Zac was holding up in front of her. But she was very much afraid she already knew the answer.

"A few years younger than Edward. Mid forties. Miss Jones, do you really think he—"

"Do you remember anything else about him? The color of his hair? His eyes?" Guinevere quickly scanned the other questions on the notepad. Zac was getting impatient but he didn't try to yank the receiver away from her. "Did he have a limp?" she asked, reading the last scrawled question wonderingly.

"No limp," Mrs. Vandyke said with certainty. "His hair was dark. Do you know something? I can't remember the color of his eyes. It was a long time ago, Miss Jones. Mostly I remember my impression of him, a certain daredevil quality. A kind of boyish wickedness, except that I think it went deeper. He used to carry a gun. Claimed you never knew what you were going to get into. He kept it under the front seat of his plane—said it was his emergency backup. I sometimes wondered if he wasn't carrying something else besides the regular cargo and passengers. But I was always afraid to ask." Mrs. Vandyke hesitated before summing up Gannon. "He could have stepped out of a film. Do you know the type?"

"I think so, Mrs. Vandyke." I'm very much afraid I know exactly the type, she thought as she glanced at the last note Zac had written.

Cassidy?

Mutely, Guinevere looked up at him. She nodded.

Chapter Eight

"Except for the limp."

Guinevere trotted after Zac as he made his way to a quiet corner of the lobby. He came to a halt, staring at the floor, lost in thought. "Mrs. Vandyke's description does sort of fit Cassidy except for that limp of his," Guinevere repeated.

"A lot of time has gone by since she last saw him. Hell, he might have injured that leg when his plane went down."

"True." Guinevere thought for a moment. "Too bad we don't have a sample of Cassidy's handwriting. We could compare it to that page out of the logbook, the way we did Gannon's."

"We might be able to find something at the boathouse." But Zac sounded vague, his mind obviously on something else.

"Zac, what do we do next? This is your area of expertise. I want to hear something brilliant from you. It's beginning to look as if our client may have been kidnapped."

"I don't know about that. It's possible Cassidy really is with the DEA. He might have decided that a career catching dope smugglers was as exciting as running dope himself. It's still possible this whole thing is a legitimate agency action."

"Hah!"

Something suspiciously close to amusement flashed in his eyes. "Oh ye of little faith."

"Yeah, well, I'm a businessperson, remember? I operate on facts, not faith. And one clear fact in this whole mess is that Mrs. Vandyke is scared of the man she knew as Gannon. She implied he was just this side of crazy. Zac, what are you chewing to pieces there in your mind? I know I don't have your full attention."

"The car."

Guinevere wrinkled her nose. "Vandyke's car?"

"This is a small island, Gwen. They can't just leave the Mercedes sitting around on a back road. Someone would be sure to notice it. And once the cops find Vandyke's car abandoned they'll start asking questions—assuming that the cops don't already have Vandyke."

"I think we should assume they don't," Guinevere said staunchly. "I think we should assume foul play. Very foul play."

Zac let a minute of intense concentration pass before saying, "I think you're right." He sighed.

"So what do we do?"

"Go back to the marina. We might be able to find someone who saw the plane leave. If we get lucky, that someone can tell us if our client was a passenger. We can also check to see if Cassidy conveniently left anything floating around with his signature on it. It would be nice to verify that he really is Gannon."

"Right." Guinevere spun around, but Zac clamped a hand on her shoulder, halting her abruptly.

"There's one more thing I want to check here before we go racing off."

"What's that?"

"I'd like to see if one of the grounds keepers or a maid or even a guest noticed who drove off in Vandyke's Mercedes. It's not in the parking lot." Zac released her and started purposefully back to the front desk. The desk clerk saw him coming and tried to retreat.

It didn't work. Zac cornered him and told him what he wanted. Making no attempt whatsoever to hide his disgust at having to oblige, the desk clerk checked with the manager, who agreed to summon some of the gardeners and maintenance people.

They got lucky with the man who trimmed the hedges. He'd noticed the Mercedes being driven off about forty-five minutes earlier.

"A yuppie dude," he told Zac with the disdainful air of a man who has a degree in philosophy but who has deliberately chosen to work with his hands. "A dressed-for-success type. Know what I mean? Italian sunglasses. I remember thinking the glasses were a bit much, considering that there's no sun today."

Guinevere caught her breath. "Toby Springer."

Zac nodded his thanks to the gardener. He reached out and tugged Guinevere's arm, but she didn't budge.

"Come on, Gwen. We've got to get moving."

She leaned close and hissed in his ear. "You're supposed to tip your informants."

Zac stared at her. "Where the hell did you get that idea?"

"I've read detective fiction. I go to films. I know about this sort of thing."

"Yeah? Then you tip him."

"You should consider tips part of your business expenses."

The gardener appeared oblivious of the low conversation, but he kept within sight.

"Damn it to hell," Zac muttered, dragging out his wallet. "Do I tell you how to run Camelot Services?" He didn't wait for an answer, but walked briskly over to the gardener and thrust a couple of bills into the man's hand. The ex–philosophy student apparently had read a lot of detective fiction and seen some films himself. He thanked Zac but he didn't seem terribly surprised.

"Satisfied?" Zac grabbed Guinevere's arm and led her toward the Buick. "If I can't get reimbursed for that by our client I may take it out of your hide."

Guinevere didn't deign to respond. "So what about the Mercedes," she demanded as she slipped into the front seat of Zac's car.

"They've got to get it off the island, and if Springer just drove it away from the resort forty-five minutes ago he can't have gone very far with it. My guess is he'll be waiting patiently in line for the next ferry."

"Which leaves when?"

"Not for another hour. We've got time."

"To check out the boathouse?"

"Right." Zac swung the Buick out of the parking lot and headed back toward the marina.

The first thing Guinevere noticed when she and Zac parked the car and approached the deserted dock where the Cessna had been tethered was that someone had dug up a lock for the boathouse door. "There was no lock when I came down here yesterday," she said, disappointed.

"Maybe Cassidy figured there was no reason to lock it while he was in the vicinity." Zac glanced around, but spotting no one nearby he went to work on the padlock with a small wire. Guinevere watched in admiration as the lock gave in his hands.

"Incredible," she murmured, pushing on the door.

"It's nice to be loved for my mind." He followed her inside, flipping on the light.

Guinevere let the remark pass. The cruiser was still tied up at the dock. "I found the wallet on board."

Zac stepped onto the boat and systematically went through all the drawers and cupboards. He found nothing. The wallet with Cassidy's DEA identification was gone.

"It was right there in that little drawer by the pilot's chair," Guinevere insisted, peering into the cabin.

"Well, it's gone now. And there's nothing else here that has a sample of his handwriting. Come on."

"Where to now?"

He led the way outside and started toward the old public rest rooms.

"Zac, do you really have to use the facilities now? We're in a hurry, in case you haven't noticed. You should have gone before we left the resort." Guinevere watched him stride up the small incline.

"The real nuts and bolts of investigative work," Zac began in a lecturing tone, "consists of going through garbage. A lot of garbage. Why do you think I label myself a consultant? I'm trying to stay out of the lower end of this kind of work. I'd like to perfect a more sophisticated image." He lifted the lid off the trash can that stood in front of the rest rooms. "But thanks to you I'm stuck with going through garbage on this job. Come here and give me a hand."

Guinevere inhaled sharply as she viewed the contents of the trash can. "Yuk."

"Mustn't be squeamish."

"What are we looking for?" She leaned over fastidiously to remove a fairly clean-looking scrap of paper.

"This is the nearest trash can to Cassidy's dock. He may have tossed all kinds of junk in here. And it sure doesn't look as if it's been emptied for a while. Our best bet would be a receipt for fuel. Nobody pays cash when they fill up an airplane. Costs too much."

They found the receipt stuck to a gum wrapper. There

was grease on it and something sticky, and a smear of gum in the middle. There was also a scrawled signature: *Cassidy.* Zac pulled out the logbook page, and there was no doubt about the similarity between the two samples of handwriting.

"Okay, so now we know we're right. Where does that get us? We're wasting time, Zac."

"Gwen, you've worked with me before. You know I'm not the fastest thing on two feet."

She grinned briefly. "But you're thorough." And when the chips were down, she had learned, Zachariah Justis could be very fast and very thorough indeed. She shuddered at the memory of the conclusion of the StarrTech case. She would never forget the sight of blood seeping from a dying man onto a cold concrete floor.

"I try to compensate." Zac dropped the lid back on the trash can. "Let's go talk to some locals who might have seen Cassidy's plane leave."

Zac moved slowly along the docks, asking casual questions of the boat-owners and maintenance people. Yes, they'd heard the plane leave a while ago, but no one had paid much attention. Cassidy always came and went at odd hours, charter pilots operated that way. No, no one had noticed whether or not he had a passenger. Time passed and Guinevere began to glance more and more frequently at her watch. Finally she tugged at Zac's sleeve.

"What about the ferry? It'll be leaving soon."

"Fifteen more minutes."

"But Zac, what are we going to do if we find Toby Springer sitting in the Mercedes, waiting to drive on board?"

Zac shrugged. "We'll be assertive."

But when it came to it Guinevere decided "assertive" didn't quite cover it. Walking casually along the line of cars, they saw Vandyke's Mercedes sitting between a Toyota and an Audi. She watched completely astonished as Zac walked around to the driver's side, opened the door, and without any warning shoved a startled Toby Springer across the seat.

"Hey! What the hell—?" Springer's mouth fell open as his head bounced against the upholstered door. "Justis! What are you doing here?" He struggled upright, rubbing his head, and his gaze flew to Guinevere, who was standing in the aisle between parked cars. No one seemed to notice Zac's actions.

"Gwen? What's this all about?" Springer started to appeal to her, but realizing Zac already had the car in gear and was forcing his way out of the line, he changed his mind.

Horns sounded behind the Mercedes as Zac made it plain he wanted room. Irate drivers grudgingly tried to back up or pull aside. Guinevere trotted over to the side of the road, ignoring several upraised middle fingers. Zac ignored them too. Within a minute he had the Mercedes out of the herd waiting to board the ferry.

"Let's go, Gwen!" He halted the car momentarily and she scrambled into the back seat. Then he headed toward the marina parking lot.

"Jesus, are you two crazy?" Springer stared from one to the other. "I've about had it with crazy people."

"Dealing with a lot of them lately?" Guinevere asked, leaning over the back of the front seat.

"It seems like it. Come on, Gwen, what's going on here? Who does Justis think he is? Is he dangerous?"

"No," Guinevere assured him, seeing the genuine anxiety on Toby's face. "He's just a big teddy bear. Don't worry about him, Toby. We only want to ask a few questions. We're very concerned about—"

She got no further. The big teddy bear had parked the

car in the shadow of the rest rooms and was already out the door. By the time Toby Springer realized Zac was coming around to his side of the car it was too late. Zac yanked open the Mercedes door, reached inside, and ripped Springer out of the front seat.

"Zac!" Guinevere reacted with horror as Toby Springer found himself slammed against the wall of the building. "What are you doing? Don't hurt him!" She scrambled out of the car.

But Zac wasn't paying any attention to her. With one hand on the other man's throat Zac held Springer pinned to the wall. He leaned close. "Where is Vandyke?"

Springer shook his head. "I don't know. I mean—"

"You've got his car."

"Yes, but that's because Washburn ordered me to drive it back to the mainland. I'm supposed to meet him in Seattle." Springer swallowed and made a visible effort to get control of himself. "Look, I don't know what the hell you think you're doing, but unless you've got a good explanation for all this, I'm going to call the cops. You can't just jerk people around like this. I was only following my boss's orders!"

"I'm here on business, too, as it happens. Just like you." Zac's hand tightened slightly on his victim's throat. "Vandyke is my client. I want to know what you've done to him."

"I haven't done anything to him. For Pete's sake, I'm trying to do him a favor by taking the Mercedes back to Seattle. Washburn said Cassidy was going to fly Vandyke back to the mainland because he didn't want to waste time on the ferry."

"Did you see Vandyke leave with Cassidy?"

"No. But that was the plan, and the Cessna's gone, so I assume—"

"What about Washburn? Where is he?"

"Washburn took an earlier ferry. He left me behind to cover the hotel tab and take care of Vandyke's car."

"So how did Vandyke get to Cassidy's plane? Did you drive him to the marina?" Zac asked.

Toby shook his head. "No. I guess Cassidy came and picked him up. I haven't seen Vandyke all morning." Springer cast another appealing glance at Guinevere. "Can't you call this guy off? I don't know what the hell's happening. I swear it. I'm just doing what I'm told by my boss. Jesus, try to do a guy a favor so he can fly back to the mainland and save some time and what do you get? Another crazy man."

Guinevere frowned and stepped forward, putting her hand on Zac's arm. "Let him go, Zac. You're hurting him."

Zac raised his eyes in silent supplication, but his hand dropped from Springer's throat. "What do you mean, *another* crazy man?" he asked as Springer warily straightened and tried to smooth his Pierre Cardin sports jacket. It was Guinevere who answered.

"Are you talking about Cassidy?" she asked with sudden insight as she turned to face Springer. "I almost had the feeling Mrs. Vandyke was on the verge of calling him crazy. She referred to him as a little wild. Bigger than life, perhaps dangerous."

"He's a two-bit pilot who thinks he's auditioning for Hollywood." Springer sounded thoroughly disgusted. "I don't know why Washburn was always so—" He broke off, glaring at Zac.

"So what?" Guinevere went forward to gently help straighten Springer's tie. Her concern seemed to have a soothing effect.

"I don't know," Springer muttered. "It was like Washburn took orders from Cassidy, instead of vice versa. It was Cassidy who told Washburn when to go look at the island, for example. It was as if Washburn was supposed to make his schedule bend to fit Cassidy's or something."

"That island you said Washburn was interested in buying." Guinevere glanced at Zac, who said nothing. His eyes were intent on Springer's face.

"Yeah. I heard him say it was the same size as some place called Raton."

"Raton?" Guinevere gave the word the Spanish pronunciation. "The same size as Raton Island?"

"I guess. Damned if I know. Cassidy wasn't what you'd call real communicative with me. He always treated me like I was Washburn's secretary, not his personal assistant. Like I was shit. I argued with him about his attitude yesterday. I was sick of it."

She smiled wryly. "What else made you think Cassidy was crazy?"

"I don't know. You met him. It was like he wasn't quite real or something." He paused and then added bitterly, "Maybe women like that sort of thing."

"Only in movies," she assured him, thinking of Catherine Vandyke's instinctive preference for the quieter man she had married. "Women tend to find men like Cassidy . . ." She hunted for the right word. "Incomplete. Empty in some way." She was aware of Zac's glance of surprise, but she ignored it. "Did he ever tell you anything else about this island?"

Springer shook his head. "No, but I heard Washburn complain once about Cassidy being hung up on the subject. Said he was obsessed with it. Kept talking about how easily a man would die on an island here in winter. Look, are you two finished? I've got a ferry to catch."

"No you don't." Zac said, glancing at his watch. As if to confirm his words the whistle sounded as the ferry began moving slowly away from the dock. "You're stuck here for another hour or so."

137

"So are we," Guinevere pointed out worriedly.

"Not quite. We've got transportation."

"Are we going to charter a plane?"

"Not to go to that island Washburn was interested in buying. For that we'll use the boat Cassidy left behind. Come on, Springer, we're going to find some charts, and you're going to show me exactly where that island is."

Springer started to protest but changed his mind. He fell into step beside Zac, apparently surrendering to the inevitable. Guinevere hastened to follow.

Twenty minutes later Guinevere stood in the boathouse watching Zac. He was doing something intricate to the cruiser's ignition system. Springer was drinking coffee next door in the small café and muttering to himself about the heretofore unknown aspects of big business. Guinevere wondered if he'd go to the police as soon as he saw Zac start the boat. Zac didn't seem to care.

"I didn't know you could hot-wire a boat," Guinevere observed.

"An ignition system is an ignition system." The words were muffled as Zac continued to concentrate on his task.

"Is there no end to your talents?"

"This kind of talent isn't exactly the sort I was hoping to practice when I established Free Enterprise Security."

"I know. You wanted class, polish, sophistication. You wanted to be a consultant."

Whatever Zac said in response was lost in the cough of the engine as it sprang to life. He ducked out from the cabin and stepped onto the dock. She watched as he slid open the metal door that opened onto the water. The sky was still overcast but the rain hadn't started.

"I hope this isn't going to be a waste of time," Guinevere muttered as she got aboard the cruiser.

"We haven't got anyplace else to start looking. If the island proves a dead end we'll call in the cops. The hard

138

part is going to be convincing them that Cassidy really has kidnapped Vandyke. We're not even a hundred percent positive ourselves." Zac took the wheel of the small cruiser and eased the boat out of its water-based garage. No one on shore paid any attention as he swung the bow around and headed away from the marina.

"What I don't understand is why Cassidy came back to terrorize his ex-partner after all this time," Guinevere said, pitching her voice above the roar of the engine as Zac opened the throttle.

"It's the time factor that makes me think this isn't going to be a simple kidnap-for-ransom deal. I have a hunch Cassidy isn't motivated by money, although I guess it's a possibility."

"Revenge? Because of Catherine?"

"Maybe. I have a feeling there's more to it than that, though."

"That's because you're a man. You don't want to admit a woman could drive a man to spend more than a decade plotting revenge," Guinevere declared with conviction. She held her wildly whipping hair out of her face.

Zac glanced at her, his eyes unreadable. "The idea is a little bizarre, but not totally inconceivable."

"What?" She frowned up at him, trying to understand his meaning.

"Forget it. In one way you're right. I'm inclined to believe there's more than a woman involved. Mostly because I don't see Cassidy ever letting a woman—any woman—get under his skin to that extent."

Guinevere's eyes widened in reluctant appreciation of his insight. "I think you're right. He's not the type to get that involved with any one woman. He hasn't got it in him to be faithful, let alone fall in love. That's what I meant when I told Springer that men like Cassidy seem somehow incomplete. It's as if something important got left out when they were put together."

She was silent for a moment, the thought striking her that she was finding herself increasingly attracted to Zac precisely because he was complete. He was solid in some indefinable way, as if there were a deep, substantial core in him. He was centered in a way Cassidy never would be. She knew it with a sure feminine instinct that she didn't bother to analyze.

"Zac?"

"Yeah?" He was watching the horizon, searching for the island.

She took a deep breath. "What do you think we'll find on that island? Vandyke's body?"

"I hope not. Dead men don't pay off their expensive consultants."

"Zac, please."

Zac shrugged, his mouth twisting wryly. "I don't know what we'll find. One thing's for sure, though. If that Cessna is anchored offshore, you're not going ashore with me."

"What am I supposed to do?" Indignantly she glared at him. "Sit in the boat and wait?"

"You should have brought along some knitting."

"Oh yeah? And what about you?"

"I should have brought along a gun," Zac said unhappily.

In the end they didn't have to worry about what each had not thought to bring. Zac circled the tiny islet that appeared on the chart as the dot Toby Springer had marked. There was no sign of a Cessna. There was no sign of anything or anyone, in fact. Guinevere glanced around worriedly as Zac eased the small cruiser into a tiny cove and as close to shore as possible. He shut down the engine.

"Do you think this is the right place?"

"It's as good a possibility as we've got. Does it look like the chunk of rock Springer pointed out to you during the tour you took?" Zac was wrestling with the postage stamp–size inflatable raft he had found in the back of the cruiser.

"Sort of." Guinevere tried to recall the details of the small island that had been pointed out to her. "I think I remember this little cove. Other than that, it's hard to say." The islet was shrouded in a dense growth of windswept fir. It was impossible to see more than a few feet beyond the rocky shoreline.

"This cove is about the only place anyone could come ashore." Zac tossed the raft over the side. "Actually, we're close enough to wade onto the beach, but the water is so damn cold."

"I'd rather ride," Guinevere declared vehemently as she scrambled carefully into the raft. The new Nikes she was wearing would be soaked if she'd tried to wade ashore.

"Hold still."

"I'm trying!" She braced her palms against the sides of the small landing craft. "You're too heavy for this thing, that's the problem."

"All I ever get are complaints," Zac muttered, cautiously getting into the boat and picking up the paddle.

Guinevere shut up, instantly assailed by guilt. She didn't say another word as Zac paddled them to shore. She felt even more guilty when he jumped out to pull the raft all the way up out of the water so she wouldn't have to get her feet wet. His own sturdy wing tips got splashed.

"It's cold," she whispered, folding her arms across her chest, and immediately wished she'd kept her mouth shut. She didn't want Zac to think she was complaining again. But he didn't seem to have heard her. He was systematically walking the tree-lined beach. When he paused to study some object near a boulder she hurried forward.

"What is it?" she asked, watching him bend down to retrieve the small item. "Oh my God, it's a Vandyke Development Company pen." Her eyes flew to Zac's. "Vandyke must have dropped it."

"No wonder. Someone was really using some muscle to drag him through that underbrush." Zac nodded toward a scraggly jumble of shrubs.

Guinevere froze. "He was being dragged?"

"That's what it looks like. You stay here. I'm going to have a look." Without waiting to see if she intended to follow orders, Zac started into the trees.

Guinevere counted to five and then went after him. Her progress wasn't exactly silent and he must have known she was behind him, but Zac chose to say nothing. He seemed completely intent on following the signs on the ground.

Ten minutes later he emerged into a small clearing somewhere near the center of the island, and Guinevere nearly plowed into him before she saw what had brought him to such an abrupt halt. Edward Vandyke lay in a huddled heap on the ground. He seemed to be unconscious. Blood seeped through the makeshift bandage he had apparently tried to wrap around his left knee.

Chapter Nine

Vandyke opened pain-glazed eyes as Guinevere and Zac knelt beside him. His face was drawn, the grim brackets around his mouth nearly white as he held onto consciousness. Guinevere saw the wariness in him as well as the confusion. Gently she touched his shoulder.

"It's all right, Mr. Vandyke. We've got a boat. We'll have you back to civilization in no time." Out of the corner of her eye she saw Zac shrug out of his black wool jacket.

"Help me get this around him. It looks like he took fairly good care of the leg before he passed out. The main thing we've got to worry about is exposure. It's so damn cold." Zac eased an arm under the wounded man's shoulders, lifting him so that Guinevere could tug the wool jacket into place.

Vandyke groaned but struggled to help them. "How did you know . . . ?" His voice was weak, his words a little slurred.

"We didn't." Zac was succinct, his attention on Vandyke's wounded knee. "Just followed some hunches. Uncooperative clients sometimes wind up in this sort of situation."

"Zac! For heaven's sake, this is no time to lecture him." Guinevere shot Zac a furious rebuking glance, which he totally ignored. He was adjusting the makeshift bandage. It seemed to have been fashioned out of a hand-kerchief and the hem of Vandyke's white button-down shirt.

"He's right." Vandyke inhaled sharply as Zac did something to the wounded knee. "Should have explained."

"You can do the explaining later." Zac stood up. "Right now the main priority is to get you to a hospital. How long have you been lying here?"

"I don't know. Seems like forever. What time is it?"

"Nearly two o'clock."

"It was sometime around ten when he forced me to board the plane. He was waiting for me when I came out of the hotel. By the time I saw him it was too late—he had a gun in my ribs." Vandyke winced as Zac started to lift him to his feet. "Shit, that hurts."

"I'm not surprised." Zac braced him. "I assume there was something symbolic about the left knee?"

Guinevere moved forward to support Vandyke on the other side. She felt the trembling in Vandyke's arm and her concern increased. He was shivering from what was probably a combination of shock, pain, and cold. Not a good combination.

"Cassidy's left knee is bad too," she said, remembering the limp. She realized what Zac was implying. "Is that why he shot you there?"

Vandyke groaned, his head sagging weakly. "Said he wanted me to see how it was. Wanted everything to be just the way it had been for him. The bastard. I think he's crazy. Certifiably."

"That's what your wife thinks too," Guinevere said calmly as she and Zac maneuvered Vandyke toward the trees.

Mention of his wife brought Vandyke's head up for a moment. "Catherine? You talked to Catherine?"

144

"This morning. She called the hotel while Zac and I were standing around the lobby trying to put it all together. She helped us confirm that Cassidy was Gannon. We thought for a while it might be Washburn. Cassidy— or Gannon, or whatever his name is—is carrying DEA identification, by the way."

"DEA?" Vandyke made an obvious effort to concentrate. "Oh, yes. Drug Enforcement Administration. What a joke. I can see where that would appeal to his sense of humor."

Guinevere was about to ask him what he meant when a faint sound in the distance caught her ear. Even before she could properly identify it, her instinct warned her it was the drone of an aircraft engine. Frantically she looked past Vandyke and met Zac's eyes.

"Damn." Zac started to ease Vandyke back down to the ground.

"What?" Vandyke lifted his head with great effort, his gaze bleary as he tried to focus on his rescuers. "What's going on?"

"There's a plane coming," Guinevere explained softly, her eyes on Zac as they settled Vandyke in a sitting position against the trunk of a scraggly fir.

Vandyke understood at once. "Gannon?"

"I don't know yet. Until we can be sure we'll stay here in the cover of the trees. Christ, Gwen. Did you have to wear that red trench coat? You'll stand out like a sore thumb."

"Sorry I'm not appropriately dressed. The invitation didn't say black tie."

"Take it off until that plane's gone."

"If I've told you once, I've told you a hundred times, your professional manner lacks finesse." She unbuttoned the coat and scrunched it into a tight ball, which she then pushed behind the reclining Vandyke. Instantly she became even more aware of the chill air.

"It's Gannon," Vandyke whispered, closing his eyes wearily as he leaned back against the tree. "He must have found out you were looking for me."

"Springer?" Guinevere looked at Zac questioningly as she, too, huddled back under the branches of the tree.

"Possibly, but I doubt it. I think Springer was just a pawn. More likely Washburn. He might have been left behind to keep an eye on things. We assumed he'd gone back to the mainland but we didn't have time to make certain. He could have been watching Springer, or watching the boathouse."

The plane came into view, its floats clearly visible as the craft banked to circle the island.

"He'll see the boat." Guinevere thought of the little cruiser anchored just offshore. "Maybe he'll assume the game is over and decide to get out of here."

Vandyke moved his head in a weary negative. "The guy's wild. Over the edge. He wants his revenge and he's not likely to let it slip through his fingers now that he's this close."

"I think Vandyke's right. Cassidy's not going to give up now. The only question is whether he'll land and come ashore like a one-man assault team or go back for reinforcements."

"Reinforcements?" Guinevere asked, startled.

"Washburn." Zac glanced at Vandyke. "Was Washburn with him when Cassidy brought you here?"

"No. Haven't seen Washburn since this morning."

The plane made a low pass over the center of the tiny island, so low that Guinevere could see the figures in the cockpit. "Well, he's with him now," she whispered as she stared after the craft.

"Thank God for these trees. He doesn't dare get too

low." Zac paused as the plane made another sweep around the island. "By now he's seen the cruiser and he knows you're not in that clearing," he said calmly to Vandyke. "My guess is he'll come ashore, but you know him better than I do. What do you think?"

"I think you're right. He knows I'm out of commission and he probably knows Miss Jones is the only person you brought with you. As far as Gannon is concerned she doesn't count. He'll only be dealing with one real opponent. No offense, Miss Jones, but I don't think he's likely to take you too seriously."

"No one takes secretaries seriously. One of these days the business world is going to regret it."

"Plot the revolution later, Gwen. We've got to make some plans."

"Such as?"

"You and I are going back to that cove. It's the only place Cassidy can land and come ashore." Even as Zac spoke the drone of the engine overhead altered purposefully. Zac looked up, but the plane was out of sight beyond the trees. "He's going to bring the Cessna down now. Let's go."

Hastily Guinevere made certain Zac's coat was secure around Vandyke, who appeared to be about to drift back into unconsciousness. Then she rose to follow Zac back through the trees. In the distance she could hear the last roar of the aircraft engine.

"What's he doing?"

"Taking the risk of beaching it."

"Beaching it?"

"Running the plane as close to shore as possible," Zac explained absently as he made his way through the trees. "It's a risk because that beach is rocky and he could puncture the floats. But I imagine Cassidy is in something of a risk-taking mood right now. I guess I should start calling him Gannon." He halted abruptly.

"Now what?" Guinevere kept her voice low. She was beginning to feel the chill through her wool sweater, and she knew Zac must be feeling it too.

"Over there behind that outcropping." Zac took her arm and pushed her in the direction he'd indicated.

Guinevere found herself amid a jumble of boulders that looked as if they had been tossed aside by a giant hand sometime when the little islet was being formed. Scraggly bushes clung to the rocks, defying the elements. The trees grew right up to the edge of the pile.

"Stay down," Zac whispered as he urged her into the protection of the rocks.

"What are you going to do?"

"Have a look." He released her and cautiously made his way up the broken jagged heap.

Guinevere watched, hardly breathing, as Zac climbed. He moved with a coordinated strength that seemed somehow out of place with his button-down collar and wing tip shoes. He didn't look very much like a sober IRS-fearing businessman right now.

Once before, at the culmination of the StarrTech case, she had seen Zac metamorphose from a conventional, deliberate, practical businessman into a hunter, and it had left her feeling as if she really didn't know him as well as she sometimes thought she did. That hint of something she couldn't comprehend was another of the elements that had kept her vaguely wary of the growing attraction between them. Perhaps it was impossible for a woman to ever completely know a man, she thought as she watched Zac disappear around a craggy chunk of rock.

Guinevere sat huddling, arms wrapped around herself, and waited for Zac to return. There was no sound in the distance. She shivered, wondering what Cassidy was doing—no, what *Gannon* was doing. When Zac eventually slipped back down the wall of rock she started violently. She hadn't even heard him. Her wide eyes flew to his.

Zac hunkered down beside her, his expression hard and infinitely remote. That sense of something unknowable in him was stronger than ever, Guinevere realized bleakly. Yet it was that very quality that might save her life today. She didn't have any illusions about what Gannon might be capable of doing. The man was not just slightly alien, he was crazy.

"He's ashore," Zac murmured bluntly.

Guinevere tensed. "Where?"

"He's circling around on the far side." Zac nodded in the direction behind her. "Probably going to work his way back to the clearing where he left Vandyke."

"Washburn?"

"Still in the plane. My guess is he doesn't like this any better than the rest of us. Probably starting to realize he's let Gannon push him into a somewhat awkward situation. I think he'll stay where he is and let Hopalong get the glory. Hell, Gannon prefers a one-man show."

Guinevere bit her lip. "Cassidy—I mean, Gannon's armed?"

Zac shrugged one shoulder. "You ever see a cowboy in the movies who wasn't?"

"Zac, what are we going to do? This is a small island. Sooner or later he'll find Vandyke, and then us."

"The trick will be to find Gannon first then, won't it? Gwen, I want you to stay here. If Washburn does come ashore, he'll probably head in the same direction as Gannon. Frankly, I don't think he will come ashore. You'll be reasonably safe as long as you stay out of sight."

"What about you?" But she already knew the answer to that. Zac was going after Gannon. Guinevere put an

urgent hand on his shoulder. "Be careful, Zac. Please. I
. . ." She broke off, trying for a fleeting smile. "Remember the image."

He surprised her with a quick, wholly unexpected grin.
"I'll try not to get it any more tarnished than it already
is. Stay put, honey."

Zac slipped away from the jumble of boulders, praying
they would protect Guinevere. He felt decidedly naked
without any sort of weapon. But damn it, he was supposed to be a real businessman these days. He was supposed to spend his time worrying about deductions, contracts, the prime rate—and how to talk Guinevere Jones
into bed. He *wanted* to spend his time that way. He just
knew he was cut out for it. He was a natural-born independent businessman.

When he'd started Free Enterprise Security he'd had
no intention of taking jobs that wound up like this. He'd
planned to be an expensive consultant, for crying out
loud. A respectable, highly paid, report-writing consultant. How in hell did he come to find himself trapped on
a postage stamp–size island with a crazy man who shot
people in the leg and left them to die of exposure? The
next time Guinevere tried to throw a little business his
way he would throw it right back at her.

Of course then he'd have to figure out a way of keeping
Gwen from letting her overly empathic nature get her
into trouble all by herself. All things considered, Zac decided, he'd rather be here than sitting at home in Seattle
wondering what Gwen was doing. Hell of a choice.

He eased into place behind Cassidy-Gannon, who was
prowling through the trees with an expert's skill. The
problem in dealing with Gannon was, part of him—the
dangerous part—was real, not some phony actor's pose.
And Zac sensed his quarry wouldn't hesitate to use the
revolver he held in his hand.

There was no way to rush him, not yet. Zac could keep him in sight easily enough, but he didn't see any possibility of moving in on Gannon. The man was too alert and too dangerous.

The breeze off the water was starting to pick up now, turning into a storm-bearing wind. The rain would follow soon. The sound was welcome cover for Zac's movements, but he began to worry in earnest about the effects of the cold on his client and on Guinevere. Vandyke was already sliding into shock, and without her coat Guinevere was going to be very chilled very soon. For now the adrenaline roaring through his own veins seemed to mask the direct effects of the cold, but Zac realized that was only a temporary effect. Only Gannon looked reasonably comfortable. The dashingly distressed leather flight jacket was no doubt good insulation.

Gannon was working his way around the island in a slow circle. Zac followed warily, wondering how long it would be before his quarry cut inland. The chief goal of this whole exercise as far as Gannon was concerned was to kill Vandyke. Sooner or later Gannon was going to want to know what had happened to his victim. If he was crazy enough, he might risk heading for the clearing before he'd taken care of any possible opposition. And if Gannon was convinced that Zac probably wasn't armed, he was likely to make his move fairly soon.

Zac waited with the patience that came naturally to him at times like this. He had that much on his side, he realized. He had hunted this kind of game before.

A few minutes later Gannon abruptly turned and started inland. There was a glint of blue steel from the heavy revolver in his hand as he headed through the trees. Apparently he had decided he couldn't wait any longer. He was going to find Vandyke and force the enemy's hand.

Zac froze into complete immobility until Gannon was far enough ahead again to make pursuit safe. Then he moved after the other man. There was no telling what Gannon would do when he reached the clearing and discovered that Vandyke was no longer there. The wildness in him made him more than a little unpredictable in some ways—in others it made him entirely predictable, however. Gannon would kill, Zac knew, without a second's hesitation.

"Damn you, Vandyke!"

Gannon's roar of rage as he reached the clearing startled Zac. He hadn't expected the man to lose control so quickly. Cautiously he moved closer. He could see him now, standing at the edge of the clearing, feet spread wide, dark hair whipped by the chill wind. The collar of the flight jacket was standing high around Gannon's neck. He swung around, crouching, gun steady in his hand, and for an instant Zac thought he'd been seen. Then Gannon continued to move in a circle, crouching low.

"You think you can hide, you bastard? Think that soft executive type you brought along as an assistant is going to help you? No way. I'm going to kill him, Vandyke. But I'm not going to kill you. You get to die the way you thought I'd die. I'm not gonna let you off easy."

Gannon moved around the perimeter of the clearing, peering into the trees. Zac stayed very still. He was on his stomach now, concealed by a clump of blackberry bushes. He could catch glimpses of movement from Gannon and tracked him until the other man was on the far side of the clearing. If Gannon went back into the trees in that direction he would probably stumble across Vandyke.

Gannon was confident and crazy. That volatile combination of factors was the only edge he'd get, Zac told himself. He inched forward, circling the blackberry bushes. His hand closed over a small rock.

"Give it up, Justis. You've got the girl with you. I'll let her go if you come on out. Hell, I might even let you go. Who knows? All I want is Vandyke dead. Come on, Justis. Take a chance. Make me an offer. I know you're not armed. Guys like you don't carry guns, do you? You're businessmen. Executives. Soft. Just like Vandyke. Bunch of wimps who don't know how to take care of themselves. You're easy meat for a man like me, Justis. Your only chance is to come on out and see if you can't make a bargain."

Zac waited until Gannon was a little closer. His fingers tightened around the rock. He was only going to get one chance.

"Hey, Vandyke, you awake? You listening to this? Or are you already dead? You've gotten soft, Vandyke. You're fat and soft now. I'll bet Cathy looks at you in bed and wonders what the hell she married you for. I'll bet she thinks about me when you try to get it up. You ever tell her why I didn't come back from that last run, Vandyke? You ever tell her the truth? How you set me up?"

Zac gathered himself. Gannon was only a few yards away and he was watching the trees in the opposite direction from where Zac lay on his stomach. It was now or never. Zac came to his feet in a quick smooth movement that flowed naturally into the throw, putting all his weight behind launching the rock at Gannon's back.

In the last split second some instinct must have warned the other man. He whirled, gun raised.

The rock caught Gannon solidly on the shoulder, and he stumbled backward, losing his balance on his weak left leg. There was a roar as the revolver in his hand was fired by his reflexive tug on the trigger. The bullet went wild.

Zac was out of the trees and on the other man before

Gannon had a chance to recover his balance. With a quick chopping motion he brought the side of his hand down on Gannon's forearm. The gun fell to the ground. The momentum of Zac's rush carried both men down beside the weapon.

Guinevere's head came up with a jerk as she heard the muffled report of the revolver. For an instant she was paralyzed with terror. In her mind's eye she could already see Zac lying on the cold ground, bleeding to death. Awkwardly she struggled to her feet, her legs cramped and chilled.

A noise from the beach behind her brought her back to her senses. Washburn had apparently been startled by the shot too. Hastily she crouched down again, trying to see the cove through the clutter of rocks.

What she saw was the flash of movement as Washburn hurried along the plane's floats and jumped ashore. She held her breath as, not more than ten feet away, he dashed past her and into the trees. There was an expression of grim fear on his face. He seemed to be heading toward the clearing from which the sound of the shot had come. And he was waving a gun wildly in his right hand. Guinevere was certain that if Washburn had known how to fly the Cessna he would have had it in the air by now. As it was, he was virtually forced to go to Gannon's rescue. Gannon was his only sure means of getting off the island.

Even if Zac had escaped that first shot, Guinevere realized in horror, he wouldn't have much of a chance against a second armed man. Frantically she scrambled out from the clutter of boulders. The only instinct driving her now was the knowledge that she had to do something, *anything*.

She was almost in the trees when she remembered

154

Catherine Vandyke's comment about Gannon carrying a backup gun hidden under the pilot's seat.

Was it the weapon he had taken ashore? Or was the gun under the seat considered a spare, something for an emergency? If the gun existed, she must get it. It was the only edge she would have. Guinevere swung around and dashed down the short pebbled beach. Her feet got wet as she scrambled onto one of the floats. Balancing precariously, Guinevere reached for the cabin door on the pilot's side and yanked it open. The interior of the plane felt a few degrees warmer than the outside air. Guinevere inhaled deeply. She shoved her hand under the seat and fished wildly. Her groping fingers touched a worn leather holster. She closed her eyes in fleeting relief, and pulled it out to find it held a vicious-looking snub-nosed revolver. The metal felt cold in her hand and she was surprised at the weight of the thing.

Clutching it fiercely, Guinevere maneuvered quickly back along the float and leapt for shore, groaning as another lapping wave caught her foot. She started running for the trees. Her feet squished softly in the Nikes but the shoes themselves didn't make much noise on the rough terrain.

The clearing wasn't hard to find, the island was so small that anyone who headed for its center was bound to stumble across it. She tried to approach carefully, hoping the running shoes would silence her footsteps. A few minutes later she knew that the man she was chasing had already reached the clearing.

Washburn stood at the edge of the small open space, his gun hand moving frantically back and forth. A second later Guinevere could see why he was so agitated. Zac and Gannon were locked in brutal combat on the ground, their bodies shifting too quickly to enable Washburn to get a clear shot. They were probably not even aware that Washburn was standing there with a gun. Shakily she raised the revolver she had taken from the plane.

"Hold it right there, Washburn. Drop the gun or I'll shoot. I swear to God, I'll shoot."

The older man froze. In that instant there was a heavy thumping sound and the two men on the ground in the clearing also went still.

Everything and everyone seemed to be frozen for a timeless few seconds. Then Zac moved slightly. He was breathing deeply, and there was blood on his face. He got slowly to his feet, his eyes on Washburn. Behind him Gannon lay limp.

"Throw the gun down, Washburn. She can shoot you before you turn around. Come on, throw it! Way over there. Do it now, Washburn!"

Something about the implicit violence in Zac's voice must have convinced Washburn that the woman behind him really was armed. He swore softly and tossed the gun aside. It fell several feet away. Then he turned slowly to face Guinevere.

Clutching the weapon in both hands, Guinevere held it on her victim as steady as she could, but the sight of Zac's bloody face unnerved her.

"Zac? Are you all right?"

But Gannon stirred in that moment and Zac turned back before answering. "Stay right where you are, hero. Gwen, don't let Washburn move an inch. At that distance you can't miss, and he knows it."

Washburn was staring at her, fear and impotent rage in his eyes. "Little bitch," he said through gritted teeth. He spoke over his shoulder to Gannon. "You fool, Cassidy. I knew I should never have listened to you. You're crazy, you know that? Out of your head, you dumb bastard."

"Shit," Gannon muttered, staring at Guinevere.

156

"That's *my* gun. Get her, Washburn. That damn thing's not loaded! Take her!"

Washburn hesitated and then panicked, apparently deciding to take the chance. With a roar of outrage he leapt for Guinevere. Zac was on top of him like a ton of bricks before Washburn could reach her.

Guinevere never got a chance to pull the trigger but a shot rang out even as Zac and Washburn hit the ground. Zac pinned Washburn with ease and then glanced around. He saw Guinevere staring in the direction Washburn had tossed his gun.

Vandyke stood clinging with one hand to a low-hanging branch. He still had Zac's black jacket draped around his shoulders. His face was white with shock, but he clung steadily to the gun he had retrieved from where Washburn had thrown it.

Gannon lay on the ground in an appallingly still sprawl. Vandyke's shot had caught him halfway across the clearing while he had been trying to get to the revolver he'd lost during the fight.

Once more everything was deathly still. Only the increasing whistle of the wind broke the silence. Zac stretched out a hand to take the weapon Guinevere was still holding. "Here," he said with surprising gentleness. "Let me have that."

Mutely she started to give it to him, muzzle first.

"Damn it, Gwen, be careful." Hastily he plucked it out of her hand.

She blinked, too overwhelmed by events to think clearly. "Why? It's not loaded."

Zac shook his head wearily. "Of course it's loaded. You think a cowboy like Gannon would ever keep an unloaded gun as a backup? He just wanted Washburn to create a distraction. So he tried to send him charging into you while he made a play for the other gun."

"Oh my God." Guinevere started to shiver. She had been very close to pulling that trigger, she realized. And she would have done it, to save Zac and herself. The thought of how she would have felt after shooting a man at point-blank range was enough to make her sick to her stomach. Then she saw Vandyke sagging to the ground.

"Zac," she whispered, "we've got to get him out of here."

Zac's mouth crooked wryly as he took in her own stunned and chilled condition. "That's right," he said with suspicious mildness. "Let's take care of the client."

Chapter Ten

"He thought I'd set him up all those years ago." Edward Vandyke exhaled slowly. He leaned back in his high-backed padded leather executive chair and looked at his wife across the top of the polished mahogany desk. Behind him the Smith Tower and the Kingdome were visible through the floor-to-ceiling windows. It was raining again.

Sitting beside Zac, Guinevere saw the look that passed between husband and wife. Memories of another time and place and all the shared years in between were in that look. It was a *married* look Guinevere decided, the kind of charged exchange only a husband and wife could have. She wondered fleetingly if she would ever have that sort of exchange with Zac. The mental image of being with Zac ten or fifteen years from now was impossible to conjure clearly, but she found she could make a hazy picture of it.

Guinevere abruptly gave herself a small shake and pulled her attention back to the meeting taking place in Vandyke's office.

"He was always so wild, so . . . on the edge in some way. I think that in these last few years he must have gone completely over the brink." Catherine Vandyke waved one hand helplessly. Her delicately shaped artist's hand was set off by a very expensive diamond-and-emerald ring. She was a lovely woman in her mid forties, with high cheekbones, a graceful throat, and hair styled in a very current fashion. Her off-white designer suit must be almost as expensive as the ring. She was also a very gentle woman. Guinevere liked her as much in person as she had on the phone.

Vandyke looked at Zac. "So Washburn was actually working for Gannon?"

"Washburn wouldn't admit it, but Gannon was the one in charge. We traced Washburn's financial background. As Toby Springer said, he emerged out of nowhere in the mid seventies, buying and selling land. No one knew where he got his start. Now it's pretty clear that Gannon financed him. Washburn provided business expertise for Gannon; in exchange he managed the huge sums of cash Gannon was making. In short, Gannon made the money by running drugs and Washburn invested it for him. A nice arrangement for both of them."

"It makes sense. Gannon never had the interest or the patience it takes to handle money wisely. He got his kicks out of taking risks, and he liked the payoff, but that was all. On the other hand, he was too shrewd to let a fortune melt away because of poor management." Vandyke smiled a little sadly. "Poor Washburn. Probably never knew what hit him when Gannon picked him out of nowhere, walked into his life, and offered him that kind of deal."

"Well, apparently Gannon had done some research on Washburn," Guinevere said. "He must have known his hand-picked financial adviser had a rather shady background in commodities-trading fraud, because he used the information to keep Washburn in line. Washburn told the police that he'd been forced to engineer the deal that set you up this past weekend. The proposal to develop the resort, the competing business presentations—it was all

160

window dressing. The main goal of the weekend was to get you isolated. Gannon had told Washburn he'd rip his new empire to shreds if he didn't cooperate. By then, of course, Washburn was used to moving in fast circles and he liked the big-time wheeling and dealing. He would have done a lot to protect his new world."

Vandyke cocked one eyebrow. "And Toby Springer?"

"Just what he claimed," Zac said mildly. "A young man on the fast track to success, or so he thought. He assumed he'd hitched his wagon to a very bright star when he became Washburn's personal assistant. My guess is that even now he doesn't know how close he came to having a fatal accident."

"An accident?" Mrs. Vandyke looked startled.

Zac nodded. "I doubt Cassidy—I mean, Gannon—would have let him live. Springer knew too much, although he hadn't yet realized it. He knew about the island, he knew Gannon had flown off with you that morning, and he tended to be talkative. It was an unhealthy combination for him."

"The island." Mrs. Vandyke pounced interestedly. "How did you make the connection? What made you realize that was where Gannon had taken my husband?"

Zac smiled bleakly. "We weren't sure. It was part hunch and part guesswork based on what we'd been able to piece together about Gannon. We knew Gannon had ditched the plane near an uninhabited island in the Caribbean several years ago. A place called Raton. He must have managed to swim to shore. We also suspected he had survived, although no one seemed to think so, including his ex-partner." Zac glanced briefly at Vandyke, who said nothing. "Thanks to chatty Toby, Guinevere had learned that Washburn and Gannon had taken a couple of trips to a deserted hunk of rock up in the San Juans, supposedly with a view toward purchasing it.

Springer also told us that Washburn thought Gannon was hung up on that island. You gave us another clue when you said on the phone you thought Gannon might be not only dangerous but a little crazy. If he was out for revenge after all this time and if he'd gone to the trouble of setting up such an elaborate trap then it made sense he'd want the final scene to be equally bizarre. We took a chance and decided to try the island. Besides"—Zac shrugged—"at that point we didn't have anyplace else to look. If Gannon hadn't taken your husband to the island we would really have been back at square one. We probably couldn't have convinced the police there'd been a kidnapping at that point. Nothing terribly suspicious had really occurred. No one was officially missing."

"How did you guess Gannon was still alive?" Mrs. Vandyke asked, her gentle eyes curious.

Guinevere cleared her throat delicately. "Zac made an inspired guess."

"The hell I did," Zac said bluntly. "I saw the page out of Gannon's logbook, the one that had information filled in on a flight that had taken place *after* the flight during which Gannon was supposedly killed. A friend of mine in the Caribbean gave me the details." He looked at Vandyke. "I opened the briefcase that first evening."

Vandyke smiled. "I'm glad you did. Sorry I was so obtuse about your offers of help, but to tell you the truth I wasn't sure what was going on myself. I got that page out of Gannon's logbook several weeks ago and I didn't know what the hell to make of it. It just arrived in the day's mail with no return address. I realized it meant he might still be alive and that he might be coming after me, but I didn't know what to expect. He must have sent it as an act of terrorism. Until he made a move, I was walking on eggs." He glanced at his wife. "It occurred to me that he was out for revenge. I wanted you out of the way."

"And that's why you became so difficult? So many excuses, so many suggestions that I go visit my relatives." Catherine Vandyke shook her head ruefully. "I thought you were having an affair. Going through the male midlife crisis or something. I was frantic and furious. You should have told me, Ed. And later, at the resort, when Mr. Justis here tried to offer help you should have told him exactly what sort of help you needed! When I think of how close you came to getting killed . . ."

"As it is it's going to be quite a while before I play golf," Vandyke drawled. His hand moved under his desk to gently massage his left knee.

"I've been wondering about that left knee," Guinevere said determinedly. "I take it Gannon was shot in the same place? That's the reason for the limp?"

Vandyke nodded. "That's what he told me when he kidnapped me and flew me to the island. Said he wanted everything to be the same as it had been for him. He dragged me to that clearing and casually put a bullet in my leg. Then he left."

Guinevere frowned. "But what did he mean?"

"About having everything the same?" Vandyke sighed. "He was in trouble with the people he was working with all those years ago. He'd been playing both ends against the middle, I guess, and had managed to make both his South American contacts and his Florida buyers angry. Gannon assumed he could outmaneuver everyone, but someone apparently realized he was skimming, keeping some of the stuff he was supposed to be ferrying from South America to the States."

"And after all these years he decided you'd betrayed him?" Zac asked.

Vandyke nodded. "As I said, he was really far-gone there at the end. The truth is I had begun to suspect he was involving our charter service in drug running. I was getting nervous. If he went too far he could have gotten all of us killed." He shot a quick glance at his wife. "I confronted him with my suspicions and told him he'd better quit, or else I intended to fold the business. Gannon could never have run the charter service on his own. He knew nothing about running a business. He just wanted to fly. He was enraged. There were other things going on at the time, personal matters that—"

"I told Gwen that you and I had decided to marry just before Gannon took that last flight," Catherine Vandyke interrupted calmly. "I mentioned that in his usual egotistical fashion Gannon had taken offense."

"Yes, well, all in all Gannon was in a foul temper before he left on that last flight. When he kidnapped me a few days ago he told me there had been an ambush set at his rendezvous point. He'd been shot in the leg but he managed to get the plane back off the ground. Whoever was waiting for him apparently made a few direct hits on the aircraft, however. Got the fuel lines. At any rate, Gannon lost power near a small chunk of rock called Raton Island. He barely made it out of the plane, and when he did he found himself wounded and stranded on an uninhabited island."

"But he survived," Guinevere said softly.

"Gannon was good at surviving." Vandyke flattened his palms on his desk and stared briefly at his fingertips. "He assumed that under the same circumstances I couldn't have survived. He always said I was soft."

"Hardly the same circumstances," Zac pointed out. "An island in the sunny Caribbean isn't exactly the same proposition as an island in the San Juans in winter. On Raton, at least, he didn't have to worry about dying of hypothermia. How did he get off Raton, by the way? Did he tell you?"

"He got lucky after a few days—Gannon usually did

get lucky. He built a fire with the cigarette lighter he had in his pocket when he ditched the plane. It caught the attention of a yacht that happened to be in the vicinity." Vandyke winced. "He made sure I didn't have anything with which to build a fire. And he seemed to know a lot about the effects of exposure. Figured I wouldn't last twenty-four hours."

"Where has he been all these years?" Mrs. Vandyke asked wonderingly.

"Playing games in the South Pacific," Zac responded. "The police checked. Apparently he was still running drugs, but not under his old name. When he got back from Raton he discovered he was presumed dead by everyone, including the drug dealers he'd tried to cheat. He decided to take advantage of the fact to start over. Took a new name, moved to another part of the world, built up new identification. Found a new business partner, who didn't have as many scruples as Vandyke had."

"How did he get that DEA identification?" Guinevere asked.

"That was phony. He must have had it made up. Probably figured that in his line of work it might someday come in useful to bluff his way out of a sticky situation with the authorities. I imagine a lot of local cops on backwater islands in the South Pacific would have been just as impressed as you were with the DEA papers."

Guinevere wrinkled her nose. "I resent that. I only got a very quick look at it, you know. Hardly enough time to tell whether or not it was genuine."

Zac's mouth crooked. "I doubt that you would have been able to tell even if you'd had more of an opportunity to examine it. It was a good forgery."

Mrs. Vandyke shook her head sadly. "Imagine spending all these years plotting revenge. It must have eaten away at his soul."

Vandyke frowned thoughtfully. "I got the feeling from what he said that he didn't start thinking in terms of revenge against me until a couple of years ago. That's probably about the time when he really started to slip off into a world of his own. Until then I think he assumed the truth—his drug-running friends were on to him—and he was most concerned with what to do about it. But about eighteen months ago he began thinking about the old days, he told me. His mind started gnawing away at what had happened, and he suddenly decided I must have been behind the setup that nearly got him killed."

"I'm sure a psychiatrist would have something interesting to say about what happened inside Gannon's head eighteen months ago," Guinevere murmured.

"Probably even more to say about me, for being crazy enough to think I could handle this mess on my own," Vandyke said. "I must admit, Zac, that when Miss Jones insisted I bring someone along to keep an eye on the proposal documents, I began thinking it would be reassuring to have someone around who knew what he was doing in a touchy situation. I really wasn't all that worried about the documents, but Miss Jones made it sound as if you might be useful in other ways, so I let her talk me into hiring you. I want you to know how grateful I am to Free Enterprise Security. Needless to say, there will be a bonus in addition to your normal fee."

"That's not necessary," Zac said in a businesslike tone. "My normal fee includes all extracurricular activities. Besides—I, uh, had my own reasons for taking the job."

"I see. Well, I can only thank you once again. And you, too, Miss Jones. If it hadn't been for your suggestion—"

"I was wondering," Guinevere said brightly, "if I could show Zac the washroom."

Vandyke looked momentarily blank. "The wash-room?"

"She means the executive washroom." Catherine Vandyke laughed in delight. "That ridiculous indoor marble-and-mauve outhouse you had put in last year."

Vandyke grinned in sudden understanding. "Pretty classy, huh? Impresses the hell out of my visitors. Go ahead and have a look, Zac."

"It's not really necessary," Zac began awkwardly. There was a trace of red on his cheekbones. But Guinevere was already tugging him to his feet and leading him down the short corridor to the executive washroom. "For Pete's sake, Gwen, this is embarrassing."

"This is incredible," she corrected, flinging open the door.

"Good lord." Zac stared in amazement at the gleaming black marble and gold fixtures. "You're right. It's incredible."

"Someday," Guinevere declared, "we'll have one just like it."

"We will?"

Guinevere ignored him as she caught sight of the partly open drawer. Her voice lowered to a whisper. "Look, Zac. There's the golden gun I told you about. The one that really started me worrying about Vandyke's state of depression."

Zac reached out and casually picked up the weapon, one brow arched. Just as casually he pulled the trigger. Instinctively Guinevere jumped. A small flame winked into existence from the barrel of the gun.

"Well, what do you know," Guinevere said in disgust. "On such tiny misjudgments whole cases for Free Enterprise Security are built." Head high, she turned and stalked back down the hall to Vandyke's office.

Several hours later Guinevere was still fretting about mistaking the gold cigarette lighter for a real gun.

"It looked like the real thing," she told Zac for the fiftieth time as she stood in the doorway of his kitchen and watched him toss the salad.

"I know, honey. Anyone could have been fooled."

He had apparently decided to stop teasing her about it and was now taking the consoling approach. It was hard to argue when someone was consoling you. Guinevere groaned and turned to amble out into the living room, wineglass in hand. Behind her Zac studied the salad, trying to decide what else to add. He opened the refrigerator door and took out some feta cheese.

"I guess it must have been Gannon you thought you saw in the trees the night you went to fetch Vandyke from the cliffs, hmm?" Guinevere peered out the living room window, waiting for Zac's response.

"Must have been. He was undoubtedly stalking his quarry. It was probably Gannon who went through your things the night you traipsed down the hall to see me."

"Why would he do that?"

"Who knows. Maybe to see where you fit into the grand scheme of things. He might have wanted to know if you were Vandyke's mistress."

"His mistress!" Guinevere was shocked.

"Or perhaps he just liked going through women's underwear."

"Ugh." She was quiet a moment. "You know, I think Gannon was wrong about Vandyke," she said tentatively.

There was a beat of silence from the kitchen. "You mean his assumption that Vandyke was soft?" Zac asked calmly.

"Yes. There was nothing soft about the way Vandyke pulled the trigger on that island, Zac."

"No."

"You told me once that a weak man couldn't have gotten as far as Vandyke had gotten in business."

"Uh, Gwen?"

"Yes, Zac?"

"Don't dwell on that line of thought, okay?"

"Why? Afraid that I'll start wondering just how tough Vandyke might have been back in the days he was Gannon's partner? He came out of that business with enough money to start Vandyke Development. The charter operation must have been operating on slightly more than a shoestring." She thought about her own words. "Zac?"

"Don't ask, Gwen." But he sounded resigned to the fact that she would ask.

"Do you think Gannon might have been right? That he and Vandyke were running drugs and that Vandyke decided to set up his partner and get out of the business?"

"You said yourself that Vandyke's a good man. You like him and you like his wife. He's also a good client. Paid his bill right on time. I don't think there's any percentage in asking a lot of questions at this stage."

"You may be right."

In the sharply angled living room of Zac's modern high-rise apartment Guinevere stood at the windows and watched tugboats cautiously move a Japanese freighter into Elliott Bay. There was no doubt that Zac's view was better than hers, but Guinevere didn't particularly like the sober colors and conservative furniture of his apartment. She much preferred her own bright reds and yellows and dramatic touches of black to this serene climate of mellow wood and stone-colored carpet. Still, there was something solid and real about Zac's home, just as there was something solid and real about the man himself.

Guinevere swirled the wine in her glass and thought about her unsuccessful plans to pin down something solid and real about her relationship with Zac. From that point of view the previous weekend had been more or less a failure. True, they had quietly admitted to each other that neither was seeing anyone else, but that seemed insubstantial and tentative to Guinevere.

On the other hand, exactly what did she want with Zac? There was still that faint wariness in her, still a feeling that she didn't truly understand him. She had always assumed that a complete understanding of the other person was essential to a sound relationship. But there were times when she was not only aware that she didn't know him completely, she also wasn't sure that she wanted to know him that well. Once again she remembered the way he could shift from businessman into violent hunter.

It wasn't that the hunter in him seemed at odds with the more conventional side of his personality, it was simply that she didn't fully comprehend that aspect of him. As a woman, she mistrusted that element of his nature. And yet there had been moments when she had felt the thrill of adrenaline, the stark sensation of knowing one had to act or all was lost. Still, she had a feeling, based on brief glimpses into the more primitive side of her own personality, that for her the sensation was fundamentally different than it was for Zac. She couldn't explain it. Perhaps it was because she was a woman and he was a man.

Which brought her back to the question she had asked herself on that nameless island in the San Juans. Can a woman ever completely know a man? Perhaps the question should have been, would any woman in her right mind ever really want to completely know and comprehend a man?

Out on the bay the freighter was nearing the loading docks of the Port of Seattle.

"Gwen?" Zac materialized behind her, his glass of tequila in his hand. "You were so quiet out here I wasn't sure what you were up to."

"Just watching that ship. Can you imagine spending your working life on a ship like that? Days on end of not being able to touch dry land. Tiny little cabins, storms at sea, tyrannical captains . . ."

"You're letting your imagination carry you away. I think people who go to sea do so because they like the work. Simple."

She smiled fleetingly. "You're probably right. Sometimes my imagination does carry me away. I tend to read too much into things, analyze them for hidden meanings, try to figure out what someone *really* meant."

"I know. Me, I'm much more straightforward." He looked down at her, gray eyes intent.

"Are you?"

"Gwen, do you want to try another weekend?" he asked abruptly.

She looked up at him through her lashes. "In the San Juans?"

"Anywhere. Do you want to try going away for a few days? Just us this time? No clients?"

"I'd like that." She smiled tremulously.

He looked strangely relieved. The intensity in the gray eyes lightened by several degrees. "Good. Good, I'm glad. Thanks, Gwen."

She'd show him how casual and straightforward she could be. "Is dinner ready?"

He looked momentarily surprised, as if his thoughts had been elsewhere. "Yeah, sure. In another couple of minutes."

"Good. I'm starving. And can you turn the heat up a little in here? I haven't felt really warm since we returned from the San Juans. My overactive imagination, I sus-

171

pect." She wandered across the room to examine the thermostat setting.

"Uh, Gwen?"

"Yes, Zac?"

"You know, I've been thinking."

"Careful, Zac."

"I'm serious," he protested, watching her fiddle with the thermostat. "This past weekend you said you wanted to talk about our relationship."

"A momentary aberration on my part. Don't worry, I've since recovered. How about seventy-eight degrees. Okay if I set it that high?"

"Set it wherever the hell you want." Zac sounded as if he was getting annoyed. "Listen, Gwen, I'm sorry I didn't let you talk. To tell you the truth, the idea of discussing 'us' made me nervous."

"I said don't worry." She smiled very brilliantly at him. He didn't return the smile.

"All right, I won't. But I think we should get something settled." He glared at her.

"Such as?"

"I think we need to know where we stand. Gwen, we are not involved in a casual dating relationship."

"We aren't?"

"You aren't helping," he said accusingly.

"I'm not sure what you want me to do." She dropped her hand from the thermostat and faced him.

"I want you to agree that we're involved in a full-fledged affair," Zac declared aggressively.

Guinevere thought about that. Labels sometimes clarified things. Sometimes they made things more complicated. "Do you think you could term what we have together an 'affair'?"

"Yes, damn it, I do."

"Right. An affair it is. Can we eat now?"

172

He stalked after her as she started back into the kitchen. "Gwen . . ."

She turned and saw the frowning hesitation on his face. For a moment Guinevere thought he was going to do something wholly unexpected and out of character, such as begin a long in-depth discussion of just what it meant to be involved in a full-fledged affair. A deep, meaningful, analytical discussion about a relationship.

But he didn't. The frown vanished and his gray eyes gleamed. He grinned his rare wolfish grin and handed her the salad tongs. "Here. You can serve the salad. I'll get the steaks."

"That's what I like about you, Zac. You're simple and direct. You keep your priorities in order."

"I'm glad you're learning to appreciate my finer qualities."

Maybe she was at that, Guinevere decided, dishing out the salad.

Chapter Eleven

The night had been a long one. No, that wasn't strictly accurate. It had been *lonely.*

Guinevere Jones glared at the stylish new coffee machine as it dripped with agonizing slowness. She could have bought a cheaper coffee maker yesterday if she'd been willing to settle for a plain white or beige model. But this little sucker was an exotic import, and with its dashing red and black trim it had totally outclassed all the bland models on the shelf next to it at the Bon. Even the glass pot was elegantly different from an ordinary coffeepot. Definitely high-tech. She hadn't been able to resist it. It lent such a perfect snappy note to her vivid yellow kitchen. Unfortunately it was proving to have more style than efficiency. Zac would undoubtedly have a few pithy comments to make when he tried it out.

If he ever gets around to trying it out, Guinevere reminded herself resentfully as she stood in front of the coffee machine, a yellow mug dangling uselessly from one finger. Zac had been very busy with a new client lately, a client who seemed to find that the most convenient time to consult with the head of Free Enterprise Security, Inc. was in the evening. The fact that the client was Elizabeth Gallinger wasn't doing much to mitigate Guinevere's prickly mood. Guinevere's own firm, Camelot Services, which specialized in providing temporary office help, had

had a short secretarial assignment a few months ago at Gallinger Industries. Guinevere had only seen Queen Elizabeth from afar, and then just briefly, but the memory of that regal blond head, classic profile, and aristocratic posture had returned in all its glory last week when Zac had mentioned the name of his new client.

Elizabeth Gallinger was thirty-two, a couple years older than Guinevere, and already she was running one of the most prestigious corporations in Seattle. Queen Elizabeth, as she was rather affectionately known by her employees, had inherited the position of president when her father had died unexpectedly last summer. Everyone had anticipated that Elizabeth would be only a figurehead, but everyone had underestimated her. Elizabeth Gallinger had very firmly assumed the reins of her family business. Four generations of old Seattle money had apparently not led to serious mental deficiency due to inbreeding.

Guinevere was beginning to wonder if Zac was the one with the mental deficiency. If so, it couldn't be blamed on inbreeding. Zachariah Justis had a pedigree as ordinary and plebian as Guinevere's own.

Guinevere frowned at the slowly dripping coffee maker. It occurred to her that an ambitious entrepreneur with no claim to illustrious predecessors or illustrious family money might find Elizabeth Gallinger a very intriguing proposition. Zac had never been overly impressed by money, but there was always a first time.

Damn it, what was the matter with her? If she didn't know better, Guinevere decided ruefully, she might think she was actually jealous. Ridiculous. The fact that Zac hadn't spent a night with her for almost a week was hardly cause to become green-eyed. She and Zac didn't live together. The affair they had both finally acknowledged was still at a very early, very fragile stage. Neither wanted to push the other too far, too fast. They were both carefully maintaining their own identities and their own apartments.

Fed up with the slowness of the coffee maker Guinevere yanked the half full glass pot out from under the dripping mechanism and quickly poured the contents into her yellow mug. Coffee continued to drip with relentless slowness onto the burner. Deciding she'd clean up the mess later, Guinevere hastily put the pot back on the burner and turned away to sip her coffee.

Through her kitchen window she could see the high arched window of the second-floor artist's loft across the street. This morning, as usual, the shades were up. Guinevere had never known the artist who lived and worked in the spacious airy apartment to close them. Artists were very big on light, she had once explained to Zac when he'd had occasion to notice the tenant across the street. She smiled slightly, recalling Zac's annoyance over the small morning ritual she went through with the anonymous man who lived in the loft.

Guinevere had never met the lean young artist. But she waved good morning to him frequently. He always waved back. When Zac happened to be in the kitchen beside Guinevere, the unknown artist tended to put a little more enthusiasm into the wave. Zac's invariable response was a low disgusted growl. Then, just as inevitably, he'd close the blind on Guinevere's window.

But Zac wasn't here to express his disapproval of the anonymous friendship this morning. He hadn't been here to express it for the past several mornings. So Guinevere sipped her coffee and waited for the appearance of her neighbor. Idly she studied the canvas that stood facing her on an easel tilted to catch the northern light. The young man with the slightly overlong hair had been working on that canvas for several days now. Even from

176

here Guinevere could recognize the brilliant colors and dramatic shapes.

But there was something different about the painting this morning. Guinevere's brows came together in a frown of more than concentration as she tipped her head and narrowed her eyes. There was a large black mark on the canvas. From her vantage point it appeared to be an uneven square with a jagged slash inside. It didn't fit at all with the wonderful brilliance and lightness of the painting.

Guinevere went forward, leaning her elbows on the window ledge, the mug cradled between her hands. Besides the ugly black mark on the painting, she could see that something was wrong with the canvas itself. It was torn or slashed. Terribly slashed.

Slowly Guinevere began to realize that the huge canvas had been horribly defaced. Her mouth opened in stunned shock just as her unknown neighbor sauntered yawning into the brightly lit loft.

He was wearing his usual morning attire, a loosely hitched towel around his lean waist and a substantial amount of chest hair. Guinevere had decided that he always wandered into the loft just before he took his morning shower. Perhaps he had an artist's need to see how his work looked in the first light of day. He glanced at her window before he looked at his painting.

Across the narrow street his eyes met hers. Even from here she could see the questioning tilt of one brow as he made a small production out of looking for Zac. When she just stared back, her expression appalled, he finally began to realize something was wrong. He looked at her curiously. Guinevere lifted one hand and pointed, and the stranger turned and glanced over his shoulder. His gaze fell at last on his savaged canvas.

His reaction answered Guinevere's silent question as to

whether he could have done the damage himself. The artist stood staring at the ruined canvas, his back rigid with shock. When at last he turned to meet Guinevere's eyes again, all trace of amusement had vanished. He just stared at her. Unable to do anything else, consumed with sympathy for him, Guinevere simply stared back.

How long she stood like that Guinevere wasn't sure. It was the artist who broke the still, silent exchange. Swinging around with an abruptness that conveyed his tension, he picked up a huge sketchbook and a piece of charcoal. Hastily he scrawled a brief message in fat letters.

The Oven. 10 Minutes. Please.

Guinevere nodded at once, then turned away to find her shoes, hurriedly finishing her coffee. She was already dressed for work in a gray pin-striped suit with a narrow skirt, and a yellow silk blouse. Her coffee-brown hair was in its usual neat braided coil at the nape of her neck. She slid her stockinged feet into a pair of gray pumps and slung a leather purse over her shoulder.

Quickly Guinevere made her way through the red, black, and yellow living room with its red-bordered gray rugs and high vaulted windows. The old brick buildings here in the Pioneer Square section of Seattle had wonderfully high ceilings and beautiful windows. When they had been gutted and refurbished, they made great apartments for the new upwardly mobile urbanites. The busy harbor of Elliott Bay was only a couple of blocks away, and although Guinevere didn't actually have a view of the water, just knowing it was close gave her a certain satisfaction. Many mornings she walked along the waterfront on her way to her First Avenue office.

Closing and locking her door behind her, Guinevere hurried down the two short flights of stairs to the security door entrance of her apartment building and stepped out into the crispness of a pleasantly sunny late spring morning. On mornings like this, one knew for certain that summer really was just around the corner. Another sure sign was the fact that several restaurants and taverns in the area had started moving tables and chairs out onto the sidewalks. The rain was due late this afternoon and would probably last awhile, but this morning the air was full of promise.

The missions, which were one of Pioneer Square's more picturesque features as far as Guinevere was concerned, had already released the crowd of transients, derelicts, and assorted street people they sheltered overnight. Without much enthusiasm the ragtag assortment of scruffy mission clients were slowly drifting out onto the sidewalk, blinking awkwardly in the sunlight as they prepared for the day's work. Soon, either under their own power or aboard one of the free city buses that plied the short route, they would make their way toward the Pike Place Market, where the tourists would be swarming by mid-morning. One particularly ambitious soul decided to practice on Guinevere. She smiled vaguely and shook her head, ignoring his outstretched palm and request for cash as she hurried toward the restaurant known as the Oven.

As soon as she opened the high doors the smell of freshly baked cinnamon rolls assailed her, reminding her that she hadn't had a chance to eat breakfast. A fire burning on the huge hearth on one side of the enormous old brick room took the chill off the morning.

Guinevere glanced around. She didn't see her neighbor anywhere, so she decided to throw caution to the winds and order one of the cinnamon rolls. It arrived with butter dripping over the sides. Of course, you couldn't eat a cinnamon roll without a cup of coffee. Something was required to dilute the butter. She was paying for both when the artist slid into line behind her.

"Hi." His voice was pleasantly deep, edged with a

trace of the East Coast and laced with a certain grimness. "What a way to meet. Thanks for coming. I'm Mason Adair, by the way. I feel as if I already know you."

Guinevere smiled at him, liking his aquiline features and the large dark eyes. It struck her that he looked exactly like a struggling young artist should look. He was taller than she had thought, towering over her as she stood in line beside him. His height coupled with his leanness made him appear aesthetically gaunt. He was also younger than she had imagined. Probably about thirty. His paint-stained jeans, plaid shirt, and heavy leather sandals fit the image too.

"I'm Guinevere Jones. Want a roll?"

"What? Oh, sure. Sounds good. I haven't had a chance to eat yet."

"Neither have I." Guinevere picked up her tray.

"Here, I'll take that." Mason Adair took the tray out of her hands and started toward a table in front of the fire. A little of the coffee in Guinevere's cup slopped over the side as he set the tray down on the wooden table. "Sorry. I'm a little clumsy by nature. Finding that canvas slashed this morning isn't improving my coordination. Shit."

Guinevere smiled serenely and unobtrusively used a napkin to wipe the cup as she sat down on one of the short wooden benches. The fire felt good, even if it was produced by fake logs. Mason Adair sank down onto the opposite bench and reached for his roll.

"I was shocked when I glanced out my window and saw that huge black square on your beautiful painting. At first I thought maybe you'd gotten disgusted with your work and had deliberately marked it up." Guinevere stirred her coffee.

"I've got a certain amount of artistic temperament, but I'd never do anything like that to one of my own paint-

180

ings. Hell, I liked that one. Really liked it. I think it might have been inspired by your kitchen, by the way."

"My kitchen!"

"Yeah, you know. All that yellow. Every morning I look in your window and it's like looking into a little box of sunlight."

Guinevere smiled with pleasure at the unexpected compliment. "I'm flattered."

"Yeah, well, somebody wasn't." Morosely Mason chewed a huge bite of his roll.

Her pleasure disappearing as she recalled the reason she was finally meeting Mason Adair, Guinevere sighed. "I'm terribly sorry. Have you any idea who would do a thing like that, and how someone could have gotten into your loft?"

Adair hesitated. "No, not really. I asked you to meet me here because I wondered if you'd seen anything, or anyone. I never pull that shade and you usually have your kitchen window blinds open. I thought maybe you'd noticed something out of the ordinary last night. It must have happened last night. I was out all evening and I didn't look at the painting before I went to bed."

"Mason, I'm really very sorry, but I didn't see a thing. I did some paperwork in my living room. I do remember going into my kitchen for a snack around nine o'clock, but your window was dark."

"No lights on?"

She shook her head. "Not then."

"Whoever did that would have needed some light, don't you think?" he asked broodingly.

"It would depend on what time during the evening he did it. It doesn't get really dark until after eight o'clock now. I suppose someone could have gone into your studio and defaced your painting sometime before then without needing to turn on a light."

Mason took another huge bite of his roll, dark eyes focusing blankly on her concerned face. Guinevere had the impression he was trying hard to sort out some very private thoughts. She let him chew in solitude for a moment before she said, "That square that the vandal drew in black. It looked a little odd. Of course, I couldn't see it very well from my window, but there was something about the shape of it that looked awkward. Was it a child's work, do you think? Youngsters getting into mischief?"

"This isn't exactly suburbia. We haven't got a lot of children running around Pioneer Square. Just an assortment of street people, artists, and upwardly mobile types. All adults. At least physically. Mentally, who knows?" Mason chewed for another moment. "And it wasn't a square. It was a pentagram."

"A what?"

"A five-sided star."

Guinevere blinked. "I know what a pentagram is. What was the mark in the middle?"

"Just a zigzag slash." Mason looked down at his plate, still half absorbed in his own thoughts. "I think whoever slashed the canvas might have brought along his own knife. None of my tools appeared to have been touched."

Guinevere frowned, leaning forward. "Mason, don't you find it rather odd that whoever did that to your painting chose to draw a pentagram?"

"Odd? The whole damn thing is odd. Spooky, too, if you want to know the truth."

"Yes, but a pentagram? With a bolt of lightning in the center?"

He raised dark eyes to meet her intent gaze. "I said it was a zigzag shape, not a bolt of lightning."

Guinevere hesitated. "I always think of pentagrams as being symbols of magic."

182

Mason didn't say anything for a long moment. "Yes," he finally admitted. "I believe they are."

There was another lengthy pause. Finally Guinevere asked, "Was anything taken?"

Mason shook his head. "No. Nothing. Didn't touch the stereo or the paints or the cash I keep in the drawer of my workbench." He sighed. "Look, this isn't your problem, Guinevere. I shouldn't have bothered you with it."

"I don't mind—we're neighbors. Going to call the cops?"

"I'll report it, but I don't think it's going to do much good. What's a little malicious mischief these days, when the cops have their hands full with real live murders?"

"Real live murders," Guinevere repeated with a trace of a smile. "I think that may be a contradiction in terms."

Mason stared at her for a second. He laughed. "I think you may be right."

"Has anything like this ever happened before, Mason?"

The brief flash of humor faded. "No."

"What about the possibility of jealousy? Are any of your friends resentful of your success?"

"What success? I've got my first major show tonight down the street at the Midnight Light Gallery. I'll be lucky if someone offers me more than a hundred bucks for one of my pictures. That doesn't qualify as sudden success."

"Your first show?"

Mason nodded. "Yeah. I just hope I live through it. I've been kind of jumpy lately, waiting for it. Whoever did that hatchet job on my painting last night couldn't have picked a better time to rattle me. It's all I needed."

Guinevere drummed her fingers on the table, thinking.

183

"You know, if there's anything more to this than a fluke case of malicious mischief, maybe you should do something besides just reporting it to the cops."

"What more can I do?"

"Hire a private investigator to look into the matter," Guinevere suggested.

Mason stared at her. "Are you kidding? When I can barely pay my rent? I don't have that kind of money. Forget it. There isn't much an investigator could discover, anyway. How's he going to locate a vandal?"

"How about the little matter of how the vandal got into your studio? Was the door forced?"

Mason's brows came together in a solid line. "No major damage was done—I would have noticed. I didn't see any pry marks and none of the locks were broken, but my apartment isn't exactly Fort Knox. It wouldn't have taken a lot of expertise to get inside. You sound like you've been watching a lot of TV lately."

"Not exactly. But I have been keeping some questionable company," Guinevere said blandly.

Mason's brows shot upward as he put two and two together. "Let me guess. That solid-looking guy with the dark hair and the superconservative business suits."

"Zac is trying to dress for success. He's learning the fine points of making a forceful statement in the business world while upholding the image of his firm."

"I see." Mason's dark eyes lit with amusement. "Unlike me. How's he doing?"

"At maintaining his image? Rather well, as a matter of fact. He's just landed a very nice contract with a local firm."

Mason nodded. "So he's doing okay maintaining the image. How about in the category of making a forceful statement?"

"Oh, Zac has always had a knack for making a forceful

184

statement when he wants to," Guinevere said cheerfully. Memories of Zac hunting human game on a cold and windy island in the San Juans several weeks previously flickered briefly in her head. She had to suppress a small shiver. Zac was very, very good at making forceful statements on occasion.

"I'm not surprised," Mason murmured. "I think he's made one or two forceful statements in my direction recently. The last time he closed your kitchen window blinds I got the distinct impression he would have preferred to have his hands around my throat than the blind rod. So he's the questionable company you keep? What does he do in the business world that necessitates all this forceful personality and image-building stuff?"

"He runs a company called Free Enterprise Security, Incorporated. He does security consultations for business firms."

"How big is Free Enterprise Security?"

Guinevere swallowed a scrap of her cinnamon roll. "To date there is only one employee."

"Zac?"

"Uh-huh." She grinned. "But he manages to get things done. You know, this isn't exactly his line of work, but I might mention your situation to him and see if he's got any advice. He's terribly discreet. He has to be. Businesses don't like their security problems publicized. That's why they consult outfits such as Free Enterprise Security."

Mason looked at her askance. "I have a funny feeling he's not going to be overly sympathetic."

"He has no reason to be jealous and he knows it. I've already told him that you and I have never met."

Mason chuckled. "You won't be able to tell him that anymore, will you? I can't wait to hear his reaction when you tell him you've taken to meeting me for breakfast."

*　*　*

Zac's reaction was forthright and to the point. He looked up in astonishment from the plastic bucket of steamed clams from which he was eating and stared at Guinevere as if she had just announced she had made a brief trip to Mars. "The hell you did," he said, and went back to his bucket of clams.

Guinevere pushed her own lunch aside, leaning forward to get his attention. The lunchtime crowd was heavy down here on the waterfront. She and Zac were sitting in the corner of a small sidewalk café that enjoyed an excellent view of the harbor and the tourists strolling the broad sidewalk that linked the boutique-lined piers.

"Zac, you're not listening to me."

"I heard every word you said." He scooped another clam out of its shell. "You claimed you had breakfast with that artist you've been ogling for the past few months. There are laws against that sort of thing, you know."

"Having breakfast with an artist?" She was getting annoyed. Deep down inside Guinevere wondered if she'd hoped to see at least a spark of romantic jealousy inflame Zac's smoke-gray eyes. All she was detecting was irritation.

"No, ogling artists." Zac forked up another clam. "Stop trying to bait me, Gwen. I've had a hard morning. You're just mad because I had to cancel our date last night."

Guinevere set her teeth very firmly together and spoke through them. "Contrary to what you seem to believe, I am not indulging in a fit of pique. I really did have breakfast with Mason."

"Mason?"

The name brought his head up again. This time there was something besides irritation in the steady gray gaze, and Guinevere wasn't sure she liked the too-quiet way Zac said the other man's name. She shifted uncomfortably in her chair.

"Mason Adair is his name. He's very nice, Zac, and he's got a problem."

Zac stopped eating clams. "Is that a fact?"

"Zac, I'm serious. This morning when I looked out my window I could see that the painting he's been working on had been terribly defaced overnight. Someone had drawn a huge black pentagram on it and then taken a knife to the canvas. Mason was shocked. He saw me looking just as shocked and held up a sign suggesting we meet at the Oven. You know, that place with the cinnamon rolls just around the corner from my building?"

"I know it," Zac said grimly.

"Well, he was rather shaken up, as you can imagine. Has absolutely no idea who could have done such a thing. He asked me to meet him on the outside chance I might have seen something from my kitchen window last night. He hoped I might have spotted someone moving around in his studio."

Zac's gaze could have frozen nitrogen. "Did you?"

"No." Guinevere sighed in exasperation.

"Good." Zac went back to eating clams. "That's the end of it, then. No more breakfast meetings with naked artists. Hell, Gwen, I credited you with more common sense than that. You've lived in the city long enough to know better than to agree to meet absolute strangers. What got into you? Were you really that upset because I had to cancel our date?"

"I hate to break this to you, Zac, but I did not rush out to buy cinnamon rolls for a starving artist this morning just because you broke our date last night."

"He made you pay for the rolls?"

"Speaking of broken dates," Guinevere continued

stoutly, "how was your little business meeting last night?"

"All business. Elizabeth is a very impressive executive. She focuses completely on the problem at hand and deals with it. Great business mind."

"Does she know how much you admire her . . . uh, mind?"

Zac looked at her steadily. "Are you by any chance jealous, Gwen?"

She lifted her chin with royal disdain. "Do I have cause?"

"No."

Guinevere went back to the fish and chips she had been nibbling earlier. "Then I'm not jealous." The thing about Zac was that he had a way of dishing out the truth that made it impossible to doubt him. She couldn't ignore that tingle of relief she was feeling, though. It annoyed her. "Now that we've disposed of the personal side of this discussion, perhaps we could get back to business."

"What business?"

"Well, I told Mason I'd mention his little problem to you."

"Guinevere." He rarely used her full name. When he did, especially in that soft gravelly voice, it usually meant trouble. "What exactly did you tell Mason Adair?"

She concentrated on sprinkling vinegar on her french fries. "I just said I'd mention the incident in his studio last night. He's going to report it to the police, of course. But as he said, they won't be able to do much. Just another small case of vandalism as far as they're concerned. They might even write it off as a case of professional jealousy. Mason's going to have his first show tonight. It could be that not everyone wishes him well. At any rate, Mason's fairly sure it isn't something one of his acquaintances would do. And there's something odd about that

188

particular kind of vandalism, Zac. I mean, that business with the pentagram and the bolt of lightning in the center. It wasn't just malicious or nasty. It was weird. Pentagrams are associated with the occult."

"You're rambling, Gwen. Get to the point. What exactly did you tell Mason Adair?"

"I told you," she said with exaggerated patience. "I said I'd mention the matter to you."

"And?" Zac prompted ominously.

"And maybe see if you had any advice for him," she concluded in a mumbled rush as she munched a french fry.

"Advice?" Zac ate the last of his clams and pushed the plastic bucket out of the way. He leaned forward, his elbows resting on the table, his hard blunt face set in a ruthless unrelenting expression that seemed to slip all too easily into place. His rough voice was softer than ever. "No, Gwen, I don't have any free advice for your starving artist. But I do have some for you."

"Now, Zac—"

"You will stay clear of him, Guinevere. You will not get involved with pentagrams, slashed canvases, or artists who run around in only a towel while they wave good morning to their female neighbors. Understood?"

Guinevere drew a deep breath. "Zac, I was asking for advice, not a lecture. If you're not willing to help—"

"But I am willing to help, Gwen. I'm helping you stay out of trouble. Or have you already forgotten what happened the last time you tried to involve me in a case I wasn't interested in handling?"

"Now, Zac, you collected a nice fee for that business in the San Juans. You can hardly complain about my involving you."

"Hah. I can complain and I will complain. Furthermore . . ."

Zac was warming to his topic now. The lecture might have continued unabated for the remainder of the lunch hour, if a small toddler in an emblazoned designer polo shirt and shorts hadn't come screeching down the aisle between tables and made a lunge for Zac's empty plastic clam container. The child, giggling dementedly, scrambled up onto Zac's lap, grabbed the container, and spilled the contents across Zac's trouser leg. Empty clamshells and the accompanying juice ran every which way, splattering the restrained tie and white shirt Zac was wearing with the trousers. There was a shriek of delight from the toddler and then the child was racing off to wreak more havoc and destruction.

Zac sat looking after the small boy, a stunned expression replacing the hard one with which he had been favoring Guinevere. In the distance two distinctly yuppie parents ran after their errant offspring. They had the same designer's emblem on their polo shirts that their son had on his. A coordinated family.

"Have you noticed," Zac asked in an odd voice, "how many small children there are around these days? Whatever happened to all those women who said they were going to have careers instead of babies?"

Guinevere tried to stifle a small grin. "I'm still keeping the faith."

Zac's gaze returned to her face. "It's the biological-clock syndrome, you know."

"Biological clock?"

"It's running out for women your age," he explained in that same odd voice.

Guinevere's grin disappeared. "Zac, what on earth are you talking about?"

"Babies," he said grimly. "My God, even Elizabeth Gallinger is talking about babies."

"Elizabeth Gallinger! Zac, what in the world were you doing talking to Elizabeth Gallinger about babies?"

But Zac was staring sadly at the clamshells strewn across his trousers. "I have the feeling this suit will never be the same."

JAYNE CASTLE

excites and delights you with
tales of adventure and romance

____TRADING SECRETS

Sabrina had wanted only a casual vacation fling with the
rugged Matt. But the extraordinary pull between them
made that impossible. So did her growing relationship
with his son—and her daring attempt to save the boy's life.
19053-3-15 $3.50

____DOUBLE DEALING

Jayne Castle sweeps you into the corporate world of
multimillion dollar real estate schemes and the very
private world of executive lovers. Mixing business with
pleasure, they made *passion* their bottom line.
12121-3-18 $3.95